CROSSING THE LINE

THE FINAL CONSPIRACY

by

Mike Rozsa

This is a work of fiction. Any resemblance of any of the characters to persons living or dead is strictly coincidental.

FIRST EDITION

Library of Congress Catalog Card No: 92-62015
ISBN: 1-56002-229-9

UNIVERSITY EDITIONS, Inc.
59 Oak Lane, Spring Valley
Huntington, West Virginia 25704

Cover by Stephen R. Schildbach

Dedication

To Ed, Carol, Pat and Kent for their encouragement,
and to my mother.

Chapter I

BREAKTHROUGH

It suddenly loomed in the distance resembling a giant piece of modern sculpture. It was barely illuminated and seemed to be surrounded by some mysterious and evil mist. This was probably due to the reflection of spray cast by the nearby ocean glistening off of the few lights that did exist. Nevertheless, the picture was ominous and to George it seemed a portent of coming events.

As the vehicles approached, a series of signs was plastered along a high cement wall. Most of them warned that the area was off limits to all but authorized personnel, and listed the consequences of failing to obey.

Only one small sign above the heavily guarded and reinforced grated gate announced the name and number of this particular Regional Rehabilitation Plant.

As it shut noisily behind the vehicles, he had the feeling that this entry was a one-way ticket to hell and that it would be a long time before he saw the outside again—if ever!

It had all happened so very suddenly that it had caught him completely off guard—to say the least. It was only earlier that morning in the still dark hours that everything seemed normal.

"Twenty-four hundred hours in the year of our Lord two thousand and twelve," droned the crystal timepiece on the wall of the crowded cubicle. George Simpson did not appear to notice as his concentration was on the small computer screen in his tiny workshop. Instead, his brow furrowed more deeply.

The computer was the latest model which was much faster and advanced than those of the 1990's. Floppies were obsolete and so were hard disks. Instead, information of unlimited quantities was stored and processed on a liquid crystal containing hundreds of advanced, microscopic chips.

The government had total control of ownership and distribution of new computers and only government authorized agents had a chance of being issued one. Otherwise, you needed the right connections and probably a lot of luck in order to buy one. It was possible to get a reject, one that had not passed their reliability testing and quality control, if you had the money to pay for it and if you knew someone who could get it for you.

Fortunately, George had a friend who still worked for the government who was able to get an unauthorized reject for him. The unauthorized purchase was expensive, but he thought it was worth it. He had then spent a lot of time fixing it and eventually he got it to perform reliably.

He paused for a minute and turned away from the screen rubbing his tired eyes. Replacing his viewing aids, he thought back to "the good old days" where everything which is now restricted and on government control lists, could be bought openly in almost any store of that specialty. "What ever happened to 'free enterprise'?" he asked rhetorically.

He stopped for only a minute longer and then began feeding electroencephalograhic printouts back into the processor which was attached to the computer. These had been taken from Amanda that morning.

As he thought about her, the frown relaxed and a small smile appeared on his thin face. Taking off his viewing aids once more and absent-mindedly adjusting the focus, he thought, "At times I do miss not having children, but the way things are going, there are also times when I am quite thankful." He was no longer sure that the United States was such a desirable place to bring children into the world.

He sighed, scratched his wavy grayish blond hair and stared at the screen again. He typed a subscript which read, "Twenty-four hundred hours, Monday, May 3, 2012."

He was not his usual disciplined self. His mind wandered once again and this time to earlier years. He thought dimly of his childhood.

His parents were well-educated professionals. He was their only child. Perhaps because they both worked, he had spent a lot of time alone and was used to it.

As he got a little older, he wasn't very interested in the usual children's pastimes and since he was awkward at sports, he tended to avoid them. He preferred instead to spend much of his time alone tinkering and taking things apart.

His parents were concerned, but not overly worried about his social adjustment. His teachers' comments tended to label him as being "different" which could have meant anything. He rarely played with other children. Yet, as he progressed through public school, he did not seem unhappy and his grades were excellent so they did not interfere.

His curiosity and "tinkerings" led to an interest in computers. When he was about ten, he decided that working with them would be a great way to spend the rest of his life. So he began to read everything he could find on them including magazines and eventually graduated to textbooks.

Although from every appearance, outwardly George seemed as though he were part computer himself, inwardly, he was more normal than most people would have guessed. Except for his obsessions with computers, he had the same drives, desires, and dreams as any normal child and adolescent, but he kept these hidden.

He always had felt somewhat closer to his mother than his father. He was sometimes able to share private thoughts and confidences with her and she would be the one to whom he would run with a problem.

His father was more distant. He was quiet and patient, but rather unexpressive emotionally and physically. George was his only child and he had no previous experience with raising children, so you really could not blame him for his lack of warmth and understanding.

Even though there was little direct contact, his father had quite an influence on him. George used to observe him from a distance with a sort of awe. He felt that his father was a mystery that he could not quite unravel. He would often sit around and listen to discussions between his father and other adults in an attempt to understand him better.

Many of the conversations were about politics. His father belonged to the older school of liberalism of the sixties and wasn't shy about expressing his views. Slowly, and somewhat mysteriously, whether through osmosis, or simply pure repetition and exposure, George's views of the world were molded and shaped by his father's outlook.

Partly because of that, and perhaps due to the nature of his work with computers, he developed a very independent and somewhat scientific way of reasoning. He did not accept anything as true or a fact just because he was told it was so. He usually had to draw his own conclusions.

After high school, he still wanted to continue his work with computers so he applied and was accepted at Cal. Tech. With his parents' financial help, he made it through and graduated with honors.

It was about the time of the "computer revolution" and his type of skills were in high demand. He was hired immediately as a computer programmer and analyst for a Los Angeles firm.

It was there that he met Amanda who was working as a secretary in an outer office and whose main job was word processing on a "Mac".

Physically, she looked as though she could have been closely related to him. She was thin and tall and wore adjusting viewing aids. Her one striking feature was a head of unruly flame-colored red hair by which she could be easily spotted in a large crowd. George thought that she was definitely not the "femme fatale" type. He was intrigued by the few conversations they had, but, at the beginning, he never really thought of her as a romantic possibility.

At first, their association was simply an intellectual pursuit. They enjoyed sharing ideas and having discussions. At some point, however, this attraction of the minds turned into a physical and sexual relationship as naturally as night follows day.

In a very similar way, their emotional and physical relationship grew and blossomed. They soon got married. This was done quietly with little ceremony.

This passive acceptance and intuitive understanding of each other was both a virtue and a flaw. On the one hand they knew each other so well, that there was no need for lengthy talks to clarify things. On the other hand, they had similar difficulties sharing their feelings so it was often easier to say nothing.

Of course George was unaware of most of this. He typed in another formula and thought, "Perhaps this variation may work."

Row upon row of numerals in binary form traveled slowly and endlessly down the screen with no apparent pattern or meaning. After staring at these for a while until his eyes refused to focus he muttered, "God damn it! There's got to be a way!"

He found himself thinking of the time he was offered a job working for the intelligence services. His whole background made him suspicious of such agencies, but Amanda had just lost her job and they needed the money so he took it.

At that particular time the intelligence branch of government had grown physically and acquired a lot more power and influence. There were offices in all the major cities of the U.S. and quite a few around the rest of the world.

By then it had become known as the F.I.A. (Federal Investigative Agency) and was a merger of both the the C.I.A. and the F.B.I. The legal limits placed on each agency were removed and domestic espionage and surveillance became as permissible as foreign spying.

The F.I.A. also controlled a national police force known as The People's Protective Police. Although it was still funded in part locally, each section chief was an F.I.A. agent and he was paid by the federal government! That really worried George!

Abruptly, he peered closely at the screen. "Damn! I thought I saw something!"

He quickly broke the loop and reversed the figures so that they traveled up the screen. "By God! I wasn't imagining it. There is a break!" As he looked, the pattern of numerals was definitely interrupted in two places and in fact several numerals were replaced by letters.

With shaking hands he nervously entered some more figures thinking, "I wonder if that was an accident or if something is really happening?" He typed in another "run" and the numerals started marching once again and in random pattern. He sighed!

Thinking back on his job with the Agency where he was working as a data analyst and as a cryptographer, he wondered, "When did I first begin to have my doubts?"

Through his work he began to realize that the agency was concerning itself with what appeared to be totally harmless and innocent individuals and organizations. It seemed to be growing in some sort of paranoidal way increasing its sphere of domestic espionage daily. When people in his very own neighborhood began disappearing, and he found their names mentioned on the very material he had decoded, he was sure that the agency was out of control.

One day he was called into the main office and fired with no explanation or recourse. He knew that he was dismissed because he had been asking a lot of questions around the office and hadn't been very discreet about stating his opinions regarding what he found out.

"Most likely, by now, I am also on one of the F.I.A.'s third or fourth priority surveillance lists," he muttered to himself. "By the time I left the Los Angeles regional office, the list had grown so large, that the chances of one's being on it somewhere were greater than not being listed! Some small comfort, I guess," he chuckled nervously although he did not find the idea the least bit amusing.

Now at forty, he eked out a living by repairing computers and once in a while coming up with a small innovation which he would then patent. Unbelievably, the government still allowed private patents! George thought that it wasn't so odd. In his opinion, it was ironically clever in a devious sort of a way. If the government allowed patents to be registered, it made it very easy to monitor those registrations. It could then requisition those of a "useful or priority nature" and steal them on the basis of national security at little or no cost for research and development!

"Boy what a racket!" he mused.

The concept of reading brain wave charts or electroencephalographs had begun to germinate in his mind about five years ago. He was talking to a physician friend who was complaining about his frustrations in determining the extent of the brain damage sustained by one of his comatose patients. "I sure wish I knew if and what he is thinking," he had exclaimed. That gave George the idea.

Besides that one use, he began thinking about all the other possible applications: communicating with the deaf mute, helping to diagnose and study certain psychotic patients, following the developmental progress of children prior to verbal facility. The possibilities seemed numerous.

Naturally, he had realized that perhaps the most obvious use of such a program would be as an advanced and infallible lie detector test. He was also fairly certain that particular application would be highly sought after by any number of governmental agencies and that its potential for misuse would be enormous. If he should ever succeed, he intended to keep the whole invention as discreet as possible, but he particularly hoped to keep it out of the hands of the government.

Instead, he planned to try to quietly market it to the few private hospitals and clinics that still existed. Although most of the major medical centers had been taken over and were run by the federal government, there were still a few private ones scattered in more remote sections of certain states.

He had started seriously working on the actual program about three years ago. At first he thought it the odds of achieving the breakthrough were slim. After three years, today he knew it was a near possibility and that the final accomplishment was so close that it could occur at any time. All he needed was a little bit of luck to go along with the many years of hard work.

He suddenly froze, eyes opened wide, as he stared at the computer. This time he was certain that he had seen something. Sure enough, in the middle of the random numerical patterns were two words—not just letters!

"Hurray! There it is!" he nearly yelled. He was referring to the two words: "blue" and "dress". These were intermingled among the numbers. "Amanda! Amanda!" he shouted as he tried to keep himself under control.

She came running in tying the belt of an old bathrobe around her waist. "What in the hell is all the racket?" she demanded. "Don't you know it is past one in the morning?"

"Never mind the time Amanda. Tell me what you were thinking this morning when I monitored you?"

"But, you told me not to tell you under any circumstance unless it was an absolute certainty."

"This may be it, Amanda! Tell me! Tell me!"

"Well, I kept the ideas simple as you asked. I thought

of two."

"Yes, yes?"

"First that we were going to have pancakes for breakfast."

He prompted urgently, "Yes, and the second one. What was it?"

"Well, I thought I should finally make the blue dress I have been thinking about."

George, visibly shaking with excitement and still trying to contain himself slowly asked, "You are absolutely positive of that?"

"Of course!"

He rushed over, picked her up, twirled her around in his arms and yelled, "We did it! I've succeeded! This is great! We made a breakthrough!"

"Are you absolutely certain?" she asked.

"No doubt about it! It needs some adjustments and lots more work, but it shows that the program can work!"

The outer door to their tiny house suddenly splintered and exploded, shooting the smaller pieces across the room where they bounced off the walls with a staccato sound similar to gunfire. Before George or Amanda could even wonder what was going on, several security officers of the People's Protective Police were upon them.

"What is the meaning of this?" George started to protest.

At first ignoring his question, the ranking member of the group turned to another officer who was standing by the graph feeder and the computer. "Don't forget to take any extra crystals you can find!"

"What about the one in the computer?" the other one asked.

"Take the whole damn thing. In fact, get a couple more men and load the whole computer and attachments onto the transporter van," the senior officer answered.

Meanwhile, George irrationally shaking with both fear and anger while still struggling with his captor, began to shout. "I demand to know . . ." he started.

"Shut-up!" was the only answer he heard before plastic restrainers held his hands behind his back and he found himself propelled through the main room and out of the house. He just had the time to glance back and see Amanda being handled in a similar manner.

Once again George attempted to break in. "You have no right to do this. I want to know why you are . . ." he started, but couldn't finish as a sound restrainer was drawn swiftly over his head leaving only his eyes and nose free. He was roughly shoved into a People's automated vehicle and the door quietly, but rapidly, slid shut almost before he got his feet in.

Again, he glanced back and saw Amanda being treated in the same manner as she was shoved into a second vehicle attached in tandem to the one he was in.

He was able to see the computer controlled transit map at the front console if he stretched his neck to its limit. His eyes bulged in fear and horror as he saw the red destination dot indicate: Regional Rehabilitation Plant Number Three.

"Oh, my God," he moaned inwardly.

Regional Rehabilitation Plants (or R.R.P.'s for short) were a relatively new type of prison. There were numerous ones located all over the United States.

Their purpose and use was confidential in government circles, but rumors were rampant. Ordinary people called them the "Storehouses", not only because they held so many, but also because once people went in, seldom were they ever seen again. Of those who did come out, few ever seemed the same mentally and none would talk about their experiences. All claimed, whether true or not, that they had no memory of the time spent inside.

The size of the plants alone would indicate that they couldn't simply be ordinary prisons. They were securely guarded, massive gray concrete complexes that covered several square miles and were often in deserted parts of a state.

The one that George had in mind, and towards which he and Amanda were being whisked through the dark of night, was right off the ocean on an island near a city called, “San Pedro”.

Chapter II

THE LINE

All hell broke out on the floor of the Combined House. Shouts and yells were so tumultuous that it seemed that the walls might crack. The President of the House banged his gavel ever louder and faster and eventually a more controlled level of noise slowly settled over the hall.

"Mr. President! Mr. President!" boomed several voices at once.

"The Speaker recognizes the honorable senator from the state of South Carolina, Mr. James Wheeler," yelled the President of the House over the new shouts for recognition. He clutched the gavel so tightly that the veins on his hands stood out, and one could almost imagine them pulsing like some strange alien heart which symbolized the ever mounting tension. Several senators resisted the impulse to flee.

"Mr. President and members of the House," drawled the almost balding senior senator from South Carolina. "I've introduced Combined House bill 5200 and stand committed to its passage. Our country was, and always will be, based on the Judeo-Christian Ethic and the tenets of the Bible. Surely, no God fearing man can raise an objection to the idea that purity in thought is just as important as purity in action. There are many passages in the Bible which state that impurity of thought is as serious a sin as physical wrongdoing. Let any man who argues otherwise show himself for the hypocrite that he surely must be. I say that we must pass this bill now. I again urge that no further discussion should take place on this issue. CHB 5200, 'Moral Thought Compliance', is obvious in its content. After all, we are simply attempting to affirm accepted traditional moral American values. Let anyone who wishes to blaspheme against God and country speak to the contrary!"

James Wheeler, who once belonged to the Republican Party, now belonged to the new minority party which was called The New National People's Party or N.N.P.P. for short. It was made up of conservatives from both previous parties. Although it did not yet have enough members to pass a bill, it was quickly gaining new ones at each election. In spite of its minority status thus far, it nevertheless was usually able to influence the outcome of legislation by voting as a bloc for the side with which it agreed most. In a sense it was a swing voter, often not revealing its position until the last minute and until it was too late for others to maneuver.

All the uproar was taking place in the Combined Hall. The two houses of Congress had been reduced to one larger one called, "The New Combined House". Although many mainstream politicians had objected to the change, especially those who lost their elected positions, the administration's argument that it was for the sake of efficiency and speed in government finally won out with the help of the New National People's Party. There were no longer any representatives, but rather, four senators from each state were chosen at large.

The Supreme Court, whose older members had either retired or died in office was totally made up of conservatives, some of which were N.N.P.P members. In spite of the fact that such a drastic change in the composition of the government should have been accomplished through an amendment to the constitution, the Court upheld the enabling legislation as constitutional.

Senator Wheeler belonged to a prominent, southern family whose roots had spread from a long line of Baptists, many of whom were actually preachers of the gospel. Money came to the family from tobacco. Wheeler had been born to that wealth and seemed to believe that to preserve his station in life, all he had to do was follow his own family traditions.

Of course he supported without question, as it had been programmed in all members of his family for generations, the concept of God, country, the family, the flag, and anything else he considered truly "American".

He believed in sticking to what he thought were the teachings of the Bible which were interpreted in such a way as to show intolerance towards anyone who acted or thought differently. He was against all minorities, considering them a threat to his values, and one could say that at least, he discriminated fairly. He was very much in favor of limiting individual freedoms as much as possible and was secretly regretful of the fact that he hadn't been around to write the original constitution. However, he did have a long history of trying to change its original intents which, to his mind, was almost as good.

Restricting differences, according to Wheeler's view, would preserve his beloved way of life including his social status and wealth. It was somewhat akin to a massive intellectual and emotional inferiority complex where anything alien, new, unusual or divergent was a threat to his well-being.

In a more subtle way, he felt that white Christian conservatives were superior in morality to any other choice, and that his mission, besides preserving his way, was to continue to work to make others believe or at least behave as he thought they should. He never voiced his ideology verbally or directly as he was a clever politician; however, his actions, and especially his political record, loudly broadcast it for him.

Thus, when he was approached by one of his long time supporters and contributors, a wealthy man by the name of Marshall Tower, and asked to introduce and try to pass a very restrictive law, Wheeler was convinced that the opportunity was tailor-made. To him it was almost like a calling. It was the perfect opportunity.

The purpose was described to him as "putting on the

record the moral precepts of his country," and he never even questioned the ultimate purpose—if there was one!

"Mr. Speaker! Mr. Speaker!" interrupted Richard Butler, a junior senator from the State of Massachusetts and a Democrat.

"The Chair recognizes Senator Butler," boomed the Speaker.

"I would like to ask the honorable senator from the state of South Carolina exactly what possible purpose could this bill serve? Surely the gentleman cannot be serious! Legislating thoughts would definitely be the last invasion of privacy and sound the final death knell of the fourth amendment! God knows that the Legislature has already violated both the fourth and first amendments many times these past years and this was done with the complicity of the Supreme Court!"

"Was it not enough to amend the Constitution to ban flag burning? Was it not enough to reverse Roe versus Wade? Was it not enough to make a federal anti-obscenity statute superceding all previous state ones? Was it not enough to have universal drug testing at random? Was it not enough to have police blockades for so called sobriety checkpoints where searching on demand was considered legal and expedient? Was it not enough to restrict sexual acts between consenting adults to the so-called 'missionary position' and only between husband and wife with any deviation from that prescription being branded as illegal and punishable? Was it not enough to have the Federal Trade Commission become the federal censor by allowing only approved viewing and listening on television and radio?" At this point his voice cracked slightly so he paused for a quick gulp of water.

He continued at the same pace without hardly missing a beat, "Was it not enough to pulverize the wall separating church and state so that instructors in public institutions can be fined and/or imprisoned for not holding daily prayers? Was it not enough to drop the Miranda requirements and to water down the restrictions on searches and seizures to the point that any suspicion is now considered justifiable probable cause? Was it not enough that a federal death penalty was established for various drug related crimes and that the list of penalties leading to that punishment is added to daily? And I could go on and on! What have we come to now? Is there no stopping this rape of what is left of the Bill of Rights? The last vestige of privacy, that of human thought, is now going to be legislated? I say that this is ridiculous and obscene and urge every member to vote against this bill!"

Wheeler was again recognized and retorted with, "Obviously the gentleman from Massachusetts must not be free of impure thoughts. Otherwise, why would he fear such a routine and harmless bill? It is only an affirmation of what we Americans believe. Let us call it a pact with our consciences, a reminder of what we wish to believe in and stand for. I again urge you to vote for CHB 5200 without further delay!"

Senator Butler shouted to be recognized once more, but had to wait as someone else was allowed to speak first. He was practically foaming at the mouth with the indignity of the offense about to be committed.

Unlike Senator Wheeler, Butler was born of working parents. His father was an automobile mechanic who lived in the outskirts of Boston. Nothing was ever easy for him. Everything he had ever possessed or achieved he had earned through hard work and perseverance.

After his father died, he managed to get through a junior college by working part time. Later, he won several scholarships and attended Harvard.

He had an older brother and sister and since they were both married and working, they managed to contribute to make ends meet and to support his mother who wasn't trained to do anything other than housework, having been a wife and homemaker until her husband died. Thanks to their help, he made it through school.

Richard was drafted into the Army and spent a tour

of duty in Vietnam towards the end of that war. Later, stationed in Texas prior to his leaving the service, he was able to observe the lives of the rural people, how they lived, felt, and thought.

He was often sent on temporary duty to many parts of the United States and sometimes abroad as a speaker and expert on "post traumatic syndrome" of the Vietnam War. He was never hurt or wounded, because he had not actually participated in combat, but as he had observed some of the carnage first hand, he had an objective if detached view and was able to help others who had suffered. He also seemed to have a magnetic and calming affect on his audiences whenever he spoke.

One day, a member of the audience told him that he ought to run for public office. Richard thought about it, and then began to seriously consider the possibilities.

When he got out of the service, he joined the Democratic Party partly because his whole family had traditionally belonged to it. He was suspicious of wealth, big business and the influence of large corporations and felt that many Democrats felt more or less the same way. In addition, he disliked certain conservative politicians and their causes and knew that they were often supported by the Republican Party.

Eventually he was elected to lesser offices and finally won a senate seat which he had managed to hold on to for several terms. Even though he had gone far in his political career, and especially as a liberal which by that time was considered blasphemous by more and more of the voting public, he never lost touch with his early life. He understood and tended to fight for individual freedoms and the welfare of the electorate.

From his perspective, he felt that the past ten years consisted of a slow reduction of individual human rights combined with an equally slow, but steady encroachment of the federal government, much like the tentacles of an octopus spreading out in all directions at once and encircling every facet of human activity.

To his way of thinking, this animal was not benign and benevolent, but rather, threatening and malignant, protecting itself at the expense of ordinary people and being controlled by some of the political conservatives and/or religious elite who seemed to consider themselves divinely blessed with unfailing foresight and the holders of the only truths which they knew were derived directly from God—as though these had arrived on the end of a thunderbolt!

Slowly, and with more justification every day, Richard thought that he was losing the battle against that particular onslaught and today was just one more of those examples!

Before Butler could be recognized again, Wheeler had called for the question. Much to his surprise and dismay it passed on a voice vote, and before he could draw so much as a breath, it was quickly followed by the passage of the bill itself, also on a voice vote. He was in a state of shock while Wheeler was ecstatic. "I guess that'll fix that son-of-a-bitch," he thought, obviously referring to Butler.

Later that night, in an anonymous house set in a non-descript part of a Washington D.C. suburb, a meeting was taking place. The sultry air, heavy with humidity, hung tangibly around the small bungalow.

Inside, by the light of an unshaded bulb, casting eerie, distorted shadows on almost blank white walls and thick dirty curtains, stood three men.

Marshall Tower, the owner and C.E.O. of Electronic Images Incorporated, a huge and powerful electronic conglomerate, and the only one which had a contract with the federal government and which sold all the computers, televisions, radios, and other electronic equipment listed on the government's products control lists, was first to speak, "Well done Wheeler. I knew I could count on you. That upstart Butler almost slowed things down, but we had enough N.N.P.P. votes to pass the thing regardless."

"Thank you Mr. Tower. I was able to be so

passionate only because I truly believed it was for the good of the country and a personal moral as well as religious obligation. You are the type of man we want in the White House, and if this will help get you closer to the door, I'm all for it!" replied Senator Wheeler.

"That's very generous of you Wheeler and I must say, that should I eventually get elected, it won't hurt your career any!"

"That goes without saying," he answered with just a hint of suspicion in his voice. "I guess we fixed the few bleeding-heart liberals that are still around! Somehow, I am going to miss the challenge of the old battles!"

"Well, if nothing else, we put the N.N.P.P.'s agenda on the record and out on the open even though it is just a formality. When I declare my candidacy, the New National People's Party will, without a doubt, nominate me."

On the word "formality" Tower glanced briefly at Sean Thompson, the third man in the room, with a look in his eyes that only meant something to Thompson. As one of Tower's corporate lawyers, he had arranged innumerable dealings, trades, mergers, and had even helped him out of some personal troubles with the law.

Thompson knew enough to put Tower away for a long time if he had ever decided to use his information (and if anyone was willing to ever listen to him), but Tower, on the other hand, knew just as much if not more, about Thompson so that it was a draw. Besides, the two depended on each other to the extent that if one fell, they both would go. The relationship was absolutely symbiotic.

A mild look of alarm appeared on the face of Wheeler as he said, "Of course, I do not have to tell you to keep your connection with this absolutely confidential for the time being! They still frown on blatant examples of conflict of interest and it might give someone a chance to get to me even if solely as an example to prove that people are still concerned with some ethics in government!"

"Do not worry, old man! I will keep it secret for the time being. After all, I don't want to be accused of giving the appearance of having used bribery either! When the time comes, I will simply state that I was, and always have been, behind the bill and its ideals. We certainly won't mention finances, will we, Sean?" he asked as he attempted to smile, but it appeared closer to a grimace.

Sean carefully said his first words, "Of course not Mr. Tower."

"Now off you go Senator," prompted Tower. "I'll be in touch."

"Good-bye. You are right. Wouldn't want anyone seeing me and especially not with you at this point." He turned on his heels and walked out of the room and out of the front door without so much as a glance backwards.

As the receding sound of Wheeler's uneven footsteps echoed eerily in the almost empty house, and a click of the front door latch announced that he was gone, Tower turned to Sean Thompson and said, "Well, we finessed that pretty smoothly! Little does the little runt know that we needed that bill for more than just formality! How about the company? Is it ready for research and development? And, by the way, have you contacted Dick Smith at N.S.C.?"

"Yes to both questions Marshall. About the first, we have a team ready to adapt Simpson's program to our uses, if you know what I mean. It should be updated very quickly, and by the time it is through, no one will recognize it anyway. About Smith, you know I keep him informed. In fact he would have come tonight but decided against it when he heard Wheeler would be here. He doesn't want to take a chance on anyone making a connection at this point."

"What's he going to do about the Simpsons?"

"Don't worry. They will be stored and then 'rehabilitated'. Smith decided not to use the old death penalty. Trial in public court might tend to draw too much attention to them. Besides, the charges might be challenged and we don't need to take that chance!"

"Smart man! Now, you'd better leave first. I'll go later," ordered Tower.

"Sure thing," answered Thompson, "I'll contact you tomorrow."

As Marshall Tower stood around waiting for a decent interval before departing, he thought back briefly to earlier and perhaps easier times.

He hadn't always been a wealthy powerful man. In fact, he was born of modest means. His large family was well-respected by the White Plains, New York community, but it could barely make ends meet.

As soon as he was out on his own and had saved enough to invest in some stock, he began playing the market. Not only was he very lucky, but he had some sort of inner drive and resolve which drove him on relentlessly. He had the dream that someday he would be famous and he recognized that wealth would help him achieve that goal. Therefore, once he had made enough to live comfortably, he was a long way from being satisfied.

Later, through various questionable real estate deals, he accumulated capital and people began to recognize his name. Still not content, he began to buy up prime properties in several major cities and to develop these into high rise office buildings and condominiums.

Still later he began to compete for established businesses such as hotels and casinos some in Las Vegas and others in Atlantic City. By that time he was married, had children, and was admitted to the highest circles.

Still feeling that his name was not a universal commodity, he finally considered that running for office would do the job. The one area that he had avoided until that point was the political arena except for quietly financing campaigns of those he either admired or could use to his benefit as for example: Wheeler.

Of course, he knew that starting at the top would be the only course of action that would quickly achieve his final goal. To him, jumping straight for the presidency was not insurmountable. For the most part, he just looked at the office of President of the United States as another business deal and getting there was just a matter of beating or getting rid of the competition. He was used to that!

He became ruthless in the pursuit of his personal goals. Seldom in his life had he been to church or cared about anything to do with religion; however, when he saw where the power lay, he quickly saw the light and rapidly pretended to be a believer. He knew that this pretense was hypocritical, but it didn't bother him in the least.

Now, as he looked around the silent room getting ready to depart, he whispered to himself, "I hope it was all worth it!"

As he closed the outer door carefully and quietly, he paused once again and thought, "I am sure it was. Soon everyone in the world will know who I am. I will be somebody!"

Chapter III

STORED

As Amanda came out of her shock and slowly to her bruised senses, she was first of all aware of the fact that she was absolutely naked. Her first instinct was to cover her breasts with her arms and to cross her legs.

She was inundated by a total lack of color, and in fact, everything about her was white. The bench-like prism upon which she was seated, the walls, the floor, the ceiling, the doors, and even the few electronic instruments in the small cubicle were a stark, penetrating, oppressive, and monotonous white.

At first she felt that she must be in the middle of some horrible nightmare. After a few minutes she wondered whether or not she had totally lost her mind. This was quickly followed by the feeling that whatever was going on, if she hadn't lost her mind, she soon would!

She wondered to herself what this was all about and how in the world could she and George find themselves in such a situation. After all, what could they possibly have done wrong that would merit such treatment?

During her whole life, she certainly had never intentionally nor even accidentally broken any laws as far as she knew. She was the product of a fairly strict upbringing in a mid-western town. Her family was large and barely able to support the many members. Perhaps that is why there was no nonsense when it came to right and wrong and moral values. Her parents, having farmed all of their lives, had no time for long discussions or drawn out deliberations. Answers were simple and conventional and that was the way she was treated and raised.

As a result, Amanda eventually rebelled against such simple views of the world and left home early. She worked her way through high school and then college. She became what is known as a liberal and at one time was a philosophy major. Even with this departure from the rest of her family, she did not gravitate to several possible extremes as many in those days did. She did not become a member of any number of very radical groups. She simply joined the Young Democrats and stayed a Democrat.

Perhaps that is why she and George hit it off right from the start. Even though they came from very dissimilar backgrounds, they both ended up in approximately the same place politically.

"So now I am sitting in some damned room, in some human factory supposedly a prison of sorts, for having done what?" she asked herself. "How long do I have to sit in this hell-hole without clothes?"

Almost as if in answer to her immediate question, one wall of the tiny room slid open and two male members of the People's Protective Police grabbed her, one by each arm.

"What is going on? Where are you taking me? I can't go like this. Where are my clothes? Where is my husband George? Please give me something to cover myself!" she sputtered.

"The accused must stand naked and vulnerable! The rest you'll find out in a minute. Now be quiet or we'll have to have you restrained and silenced now," answered one of the men.

She was led and partially dragged down an endless white corridor which had seemingly no doors nor windows although there was a sign, once in a while, perhaps indicating some hidden panels or additional rooms. They finally stopped at one marked, "People's Internal Court Number Three."

One of the officers placed his index finger into a

hole in the otherwise unbroken surface of the endless white wall, and almost immediately, and as Amanda had suspected, a hitherto unseen panel slid back with a whooshing sound.

She was roughly shoved through the opening and immediately became aware of several other people in the room. One was an official dressed totally in a black uniform which contrasted eerily against the absolute whiteness of the room. Her eyes landed on George, also naked, and restrained both at the wrists and so that he could not speak, and he too was flanked by two guards of the People's Police.

Amanda just had time to shout, "George, Oh, George! What is . . ." before restraints were placed over her head and on her wrists. She was stopped on the other side of the room from George and in front of some sort of machine or computer. The machine had two large buttons, one red marked, "Yes" and one black labeled, "No". Amanda could guess their general purpose without even being told.

The man in the black uniform, who was behind a large tall white desk, spoke after a couple of seconds, "For your information, I am Judge Stevens! You have been accused of several crimes against the people of the United States and the State of California. I will tell you of your rights and then we shall proceed with the documentation trial. Guards, you may release one hand of each of the accused."

"You have the right to answer all questions put to you by pressing either the black button or the red button. In front of you are People's Evidence Machines. They will record your responses and will provide evidence of these proceedings. Be careful that your answers are correct or further violations will be recorded against you in the form of perjury! Do you understand?"

Both Amanda and George, hesitatingly and reluctantly pushed their red buttons. Amanda wondered what had happened to the jury, the lawyers, the recorder, her rights, and in fact, she had absolutely no idea of what they were being accused; however, she had the feeling she was about to find out!

As if reading her mind, the judge said, "You are in violation of Penal Code Section 2319 of the state of California, Sections 2a and 3b, and Federal Statutes 3456, Sections 38d and 38e. To wit: to have knowingly and openly taken possession of equipment on the government's controlled lists without proper authorization and registration; having attempted to use said equipment for personal monetary gain as well as the development of programs which could jeopardize the security of the United States; to have openly questioned the policies of both the State of California and the federal government and to have voiced these criticisms openly and blatantly once again endangering the security of the United States. How do you plead?"

Amanda and George seemed immobilized. With the expression of fear showing in the parts of the eyes that were visible, neither moved a muscle.

The judge shouted, "Perhaps you did not hear me? Press the button for your plea! 'Yes' for guilty or 'No' for not guilty!"

This time their free hand shot out and landed on the black button of their respective machine so fast that if anyone had blinked they would have missed it.

"So be it," remarked the judge. "Let the trial begin. You will answer either 'Yes' or 'No' to each of the questions which I shall pose and in the manner which we have already discussed. The first question is: Did George Simpson acquire a government restricted computer through channels other than those proscribed by the regulations and was so aided in doing so by your wife Amanda?"

George glanced at Amanda who looked back at him. She shrugged her shoulders at which point the judge interjected, "There will be no, I repeat, no communication between the defendants! If you again attempt such behavior, not only will further charges be filed, but we will have to restrict your physical movements and restrain you even further. Now, answer the question, both of you!"

George slowly reached for the red button and pressed it with Amanda following suit.

"Now, did you openly and blatantly criticize the United States Government at your work area before you were fired, and, aided by Mrs. Simpson, do so in public places after you were relieved of your job, and further do so to various friends and acquaintances in your neighborhood?"

George pressed the red button while Amanda hesitated and then did so too.

"Did both you and your wife Amanda participate in using the unauthorized computer to develop programs and sell same for monetary gain?"

They both pressed the red buttons.

"Did you Mr. Simpson, and you Mrs. Simpson, participate in experiments upon said computer where you attempted to develop a program which could translate brain waves into readable thought? Furthermore, using the assumption that you usually sold your programs for personal gain, is it not possible to presume that if sold to the wrong people, and should it have fallen into enemy hands, it could have been of great detriment to the security of the United States?"

"Why in the hell are you asking me since you seem to know all the answers?" asked George to himself. "Obviously, they must have had the house thoroughly bugged for a long time as I rather suspected. I object to the last part of that question, but I am stuck!" He pushed the red button and Amanda hesitantly did the same.

"Having concluded the questioning, I will now ask the guards at each of the machines to unlock and push the 'verdict button'," announced the judge.

As they watched in fascinated curiosity mixed with barely controllable fear, the computer-like machine hummed for a couple of seconds and then spewed out a relatively small piece of computer paper. The run was fast and rather short, leading to the conclusion that the answer was simple and perhaps with little supporting explanation.

"If the guards will hand me the verdicts, I shall read them out loud prior to pronouncing sentence," announced the judge.

"Sentence? He sounds as though he already knows the verdict! Unfortunately, I have the awful feeling that there is only one verdict allowed on these damned machines!" thought Amanda.

George as well was thinking, "This is a God damned set-up! Those lousy bastards control the whole process! Some court! Some fucking justice! They just want us put away! Threat to national security, bullshit! They just want us out of the way! I bet they want my program! I am sure it has something to do with that! I was always afraid it would fall in the wrong hands, but little did I imagine it happening this way! God, this is awful! We are totally powerless. No wonder people seldom come out of these concrete traps!"

The judge's voice interrupted George's thoughts with, "The verdict reads as follows: George Simpson guilty as charged, having answered 'Yes' to all questions posed. Amanda Simpson guilty as charged, having answered 'Yes' to all questions asked."

He continued, "I now sentence you, George Simpson, on this twenty-third day of May, in the year of our Lord two thousand twelve, to four and one half years of storage in this Regional Rehabilitation Plant with final intensive rehabilitation before separation. I sentence you, Amanda Simpson, to the same four and one half years of incarceration in this R.R.P. to include equally intensive final rehabilitation. You may escort the prisoners back to their respective life-supporting cubicles and prepare them for storage."

Both Amanda's and George's eyes reflected the final

terror of those terrible pronouncements as, struggling and resisting once more, they were finally dragged off.

The judge, left alone, superfluously slammed his hand onto a large button on his desk and proclaimed in words that bounced off the walls of the now empty white room, "This court is adjourned!"

Chapter IV

CROSSING

Senator Harry Owens was an upstanding citizen. He was elected from the state of Ohio and had an impeccable record. He had a nice family, a nice home, and a great reputation.

Unfortunately, he had one weakness—he had upon occasion "strayed from the nest" so to speak. Once in a great while, he had an uncontrollable urge to make mad, passionate love to a much younger girl.

To date he had gotten away with it completely and no one had the slightest hint of any irregularity. He used a very dependable service and had done so for many years. He absolutely could count on their discretion and, of course, those who ran the service were well rewarded.

Politically, he among others, had also undertaken the task of opposing the N.N.P.P.'s large agenda by voting against most of its proposals even though the effort was almost always futile. The biggest task of all still lay ahead, and that consisted of opposing the newly announced N.N.P.P.'s candidate for the office of President of the United States. Owens vowed to lay his life down, if need be, to stop Marshall Tower from getting to that high office. He wasn't sure how he was going to do it, but he was ready to try every dirty trick he could muster if need be. It was therefore imperative that he lead a circumspect personal life as any public hint of scandal would render him totally impotent politically.

He was desperate, both in finding a way to stop Tower and at the moment for the satisfaction of his own desires. He realized that to give in to his recent urges would be like walking a tightrope where at any moment he might falter and then fall. In some ways, this conflict added to the tension, excitement and feelings of longing. It was very much like a little child who wants something even more because he has been told that he can't have it.

As he paced his hotel room heatedly and became drenched in sweat, he couldn't seem to make up his mind. He knew that he should not give in and should think about his reputation. He was afraid to imagine as well the consequences to his family if he were caught.

On the other hand, that yearning in his gut, that old feeling which had been neglected for a long time was gnawing at him constantly. Even when he tried to sleep desperate dreams would snap him back to wakefulness and increase his longings to the point that all rationality was close to being lost.

With a snap of his fingers, the video screen which was framed and set into the wall, came alive, but he immediately ignored the three dimensional pictures and stereo sound emanating from it.

"Christ! I just can't do it!" he moaned to himself. "Supposing someone were to find out this time. I just can't take that chance! I have the feeling that they are just waiting for one false move to nail me. Still no one ever found out before. Why should it be so different this time? All I know is that I want some young smooth thing that is fresh and alive with passion to have and to hold for just a little while. Helen was that way once, but no more! Now, if she condescends, she just lies there without so much as moving a muscle as if she were doing me some big favor or as if it were part of her household chores. Who needs that?"

He began pacing the floor again, paused in front of the videophone, pressed the call button, pressed the cancel button, and then began pacing again when there suddenly came a loud knock on the outer door.

"Christ, I hear you! Hold on to your shirt! I'll be right there!" he commented as he started for the door. Before he took one full step, the door came crashing off its hinges and fell inward barely avoiding hitting him on the head.

"What the hell . . ." he started to say as he was quickly grabbed by two members of the People's Protective Police.

"Senator Owens, in the name of the People, I arrest you under section 6a of the Federal Combined House Bill 5200!" droned one of the officers.

"What the hell are you talking about? I haven't done anything illegal! You guys must be insane!" sputtered Owens. "Bill 5200 baloney! That was just a formality! Everyone knows that! You can't know what I've been thinking and that's for sure!"

"You can tell that to the judge of Regional Rehabilitation Plant Number One," answered the other member of the People's Police and with that statement Senator Owens was restrained both head and hands and dragged off emitting muffled cries of desperation.

* * *

"How did I get myself into this mess?" Emma Chandler, a menopausal, wealthy, and socially prominent wife of a famous surgeon and expert in human bionic replacements, thought to herself. "At my age to be caught in such a position! It was only a one-time affair and I thought I was as safe as they come. Can't tell Tom, he'd never understand. I just cannot have the baby, and that's all there is to it. Abortions are illegal, but perhaps I could find some discreet way of doing it with no one finding out. Yes, that's got to be the solution."

She was sitting on a chaise near the pool of her multi-million dollar estate outside of Austin, Texas contemplating her predicament. She switched on the video screen which was hanging from a cart-like vehicle with a snap of her fingers and for a while was absorbed in the news of the day.

She smiled sarcastically at the appearance on the

screen of Marshall Tower, sweating under the noonday sun of Los Angeles and addressing a crowd of supporters. He looked tired and seemed to have lost some of his outward veneer of invulnerability.

"Anyone who would vote for that son-of-a-bitch would have to be crazy," she said half-aloud.

Mrs. Chandler had been a large contributor of the opposite party and so had her husband. Not only did she not like Tower personally, she and her husband disliked his business practices. They had been deprived of a lucrative real estate deal that was all but concluded when Tower and his cronies had somehow managed to undercut the deal by offering more money and by pulling some strings.

Mr. Chandler might have let "bygones be bygones", but she was not so forgiving. She had consequently poured a fortune into the coffers of the opposition party's candidate.

Leaving the screen for a minute, Emma thought again about her more immediate problem. She had a friend who had had an abortion a couple of years ago and everything was fine. Of course the laws were even more strict now, but perhaps she could still get away with it. "That's it. I'll call Joan tonight and arrange to meet with her," she decided.

Having settled her next move for the moment, Emma settled back on her lounge, took a sip of a tall drink and turned her attention back to the screen. It was at that moment that she felt strong arms grasping her shoulders and lifting her out of her chaise.

She screamed with surprise before she realized there was more to worry about. She was whisked off in a People's conveyance vehicle to Regional Rehabilitation Plant Number Eight before she could utter more than a vain protest.

* * *

A dark unmarked transporter van slowly cruised by the ultra secure condominium complex not very far from Hollywood Boulevard. Following at a discreet distance was a marked People's conveyance vehicle. The large transporter slowly worked its way around the complex and then continued to circle at an even pace. It obviously was on automatic and must have had some sort of clearance from Traffic Central as otherwise it would have been stopped at each corner of the complex by lazer intersection control beams.

Inside one of the large luxurious units was Senator Fred Morton just back from Washington and on a break during a short recess of the New Combined House. He was one of those few liberal senators left in the House and he too had been battling the N.N.P.P.'s attempts at legislation. He and Senator Butler often conferred and planned out their strategy.

He had grown up in Hollywood and kept this condominium partly out of nostalgia for the old days.

"Whew! It's good to be quiet and out of the rat race for a while," he said soothingly to himself. "Now if only I could find some way of getting laid without anyone finding out about it, my short vacation would be complete."

Senator Morton thought back and tried to remember the last time he had had sex, "It's been so long that I can't even remember!"

Contrary to Senator Owens, Morton was not looking for a young girl, but rather, a young man. Nevertheless, he was in about the same, or perhaps even a worse predicament, as homosexuality was totally against the law as was any form of sexual conduct other than the "prescribed" one between husband and wife.

"Some of the old bars must still exist," he mumbled to no one in particular. He snapped his fingers and the video screen, inlaid into the wall of the living room, came to life with sputterings of sound and flashes of color. He passed his hand over an invisible beam on a small table next to the couch and the channels flipped as if by magic.

"I must take a chance and find a trick," he thought. "I know. I'll dress so that no one could possibly recognize me and see if I can find one of the bars that used to exist in this area. They could at least let me know how to meet a man or a boy these days."

He rushed into the bedroom, threw off his outer garments, rummaged through his closet, found an old holey pair of jeans, a non-descript sweatshirt, some sneakers, an old baseball cap, and turning to a dresser he pulled out a pair of dark glasses.

Glancing at himself in the mirror he thought, "Perfect. No one would ever think they were looking at a Senator." Looking back at him was a youngish, middle-aged, well-built man of regular facial features. He could have passed for a man of thirty, and he had definitely achieved total anonymity.

Tying his laces on the run, he hopped across the living room, snapped off the videoscreen, opened the outer door and ran smack into several officers of the People's Protective Police.

* * *

From the outside, the transporter looked like any other van. One would have assumed that it was carrying routine equipment or even furniture although its black color was somewhat unusual and so was the fact that it had no markings. Had one looked carefully, one would have noticed extra antennae and camouflaged electronic dishes which were far more numerous than those needed for simple laser traffic routings, radar, or normal communications.

The semi-fluorescent humming and flashing interior was an altogether different matter. It was the type of scene found usually in futuristic movies and seldom seen by the common eye. The whole left wall was filled from floor to ceiling with polygraph-like machines including styluses and graph paper and each machine was labeled with what appeared to be a person's name. The right wall was equally filled with advanced audio recorders and each machine held a shiny new laser disc easily recognizable as those used for recording sound. These also had labels with names of people on them.

Dominating the floor space between the two walls was an enormous electronic console that somewhat resembled a U.F.O. and gave the impression that it would soon be taking off for outer space.

Darting from the console to one of the walls and back again and on to the next wall and back were three men in white coats. Each had an N.S.C. tag showing his name and the type of clearance each was allowed. Every once in a while, one of the men would tear off an active graph, run over to the console and feed it in and then carefully monitor the results on one of the many videoscreens.

This time he shook his head and simply said, "No good! We need a better graph for final evidence. Anything verbal coming in?"

One of the technicians pushed a button on the audio recorder, listened for a minute, shook his head and said, "Nothing out loud yet either. We'll just keep monitoring until we nail him. This guy's a tough one!"

This time the van was cruising around a fashionable Washington suburb where many of the wealthy and the politically powerful lived.

Inside one of the less pretentious mansions Senator Larry Johnson was trying to relax in his study. He had just had a very trying day debating Senator Wheeler and he was exhausted. His wife came in and asked if he needed anything.

"No honey. Just do me the favor of keeping the kids away and not letting anyone disturb me for a while. O.K.?" he asked.

"Anything you say dear. Let me know when you will be ready for dinner," and with that she left closing the door gently behind her.

He thought back on the day with something close to disgust. "Can't even argue with that son-of-a-bitch! Who can win an argument against the invocation of God, Mary, Jesus and practically the Holy Ghost?"

He snapped on the videoscreen set in the wall between shelves of books. A smiling Tower drawled on, "I am the candidate of the people! I will look out for the little guy! I will be the only one who will reduce taxes!"

"My ass you will! Who could possibly believe all that shit?" Johnson thought to himself. "Unfortunately, the real answer is too many may!" He flipped the channel.

" . . . and the day of reckoning is upon us. God almighty shall punish those who do not follow His rules. It is written that ye . . ."

He flipped the channel again thinking, "I had to listen to all that crap in the Combined House today, and now I get it on television. When are they ever going to learn that there is no such thing as a god! You would have thought after all these thousands of years of history more people would have awakened to that fact. Instead the number of atheists dwindles every day. Something I just can't understand, but wish I could do something about! You would have thought that television evangelism would have been finished with the scandals of the nineties, but no. How soon everyone forgets!"

Back in the van one of the technicians shot straight into the air and let out a whoop, "Finally, we've got him. He is an atheist just as we suspected all along." In his hand he held the graph paper that had been torn off of one of the machines labeled, "Senator Johnson".

"Make contact with the conveyance vehicle and have him picked up!"

* * *

Joel was working his way towards downtown Chicago. He had managed to find some relatively decent clothes and had found a way under the fence that divided the homeless and indigent from the rest of the population.

As a matter of fact, even though there were large populations of the homeless in all the major cities, these were almost never seen by the average working citizen. Once you were not able to support and house yourself, you were segregated into modern ghettos, usually found in the old warehouses and abandoned factories sections of town. These compounds were heavily guarded and no one without a pass was allowed to leave.

Whatever happened inside, however, was of nobody's concern and an unwritten agreement existed wherein the authorities hoped that much of the population would either kill each other off or die from disease or starvation or any combination thereof.

Getting a pass out was almost impossible. You had to have a sponsor who could vouch for you and who was willing not only to house you, but to guarantee that you would have steady employment.

There was one other unwritten rule among the people in charge and that was that another quick way to reduce the undesirable population was to take some of them to the nearest R.R.P. This was especially true if the restricted areas got so overcrowded that there was the danger that some of the people might spill out into the "normal" population.

As Joel continued to walk on down the street, he was trying hard to think of someone he might be able to find who could help him. He had to get off the streets and into shelter by night fall or he knew he would be in trouble.

He had once held a relatively good job as a clerk and seemed to be doing just fine until his child got sick. The doctor bills put him into debt and, since all forms of government assistance had by that time disappeared, he had nowhere to turn.

When his wife got extremely ill as well, he missed many days of work and was eventually fired. Both his son and his wife soon passed away and for a long time, he didn't even care about his own condition. Since he was unemployed, he soon found himself on the street and quickly thereafter in the restricted area.

Today, however, he was recovering from his depression and finally determined to try and join the regular civilians once more.

He suddenly tensed. He passed a couple of members of the People's Protective Police. They didn't even seem to notice him. With a sigh of relief he walked on when he suddenly felt something in his pocket. "I'll be darned," he exclaimed. "A cigarette. Haven't seen one of those for a long time."

Somehow he had hung onto his electronic flamer through all his experiences. It was given to him by his wife on their last anniversary together. He pulled it out, quickly lit the cigarette, and took a long drag from it. No sooner had he let out the smoke than he was stopped by the People's Protective Police with one of them stating, "You are under arrest for possession and use of tobacco mister!"

* * *

A Democratic precinct worker was arrested for contemplating suicide.

The son of a prominent, liberal defense lawyer was taken in for pornographic daydreams.

A factory worker received the death penalty for possessing a half kilo of marijuana.

The co-chairman of the Democratic National Committee was detained for thinking about making a cocktail with his aftershave lotion.

The president of the National A.C.L.U. was stopped after making a speech on the rights of privacy in general and in specifically advocating a right to die.

An artist was incarcerated for thinking about making a painting which included nudes.

A woman was arrested for contemplating returning to her old line of work—prostitution.

A college student was stopped after having read parts of Shakespeare that were not on the government's approved list.

And the silent shiny black transporter van cruised on . . . .

Chapter V

TIGHTENING

Barely visible shadowy figures moved silently in the inky blackness and gravitated towards an old dusty and almost forgotten storage room at the old Executive Office Building.

First to slip in was Dick Smith, the National Security Director, who quickly pulled the blinds before turning on a light. He could feel his heart pounding in his throat at the anticipation of setting in motion all those plans and dreams for which he had dedicated his life. He was also slightly concerned that the opportunity might suddenly be wrenched from his grasp should he have a heart attack. This he dismissed as nonsense and nothing but a simple case of nerves. He forced himself to breathe slowly and calmly and soon his anxiety abated to a controlable degree.

In many ways his background and outlook were very much like those of Senator Wheeler. He was an only child of a wealthy southern family, had been brought up in a very strict and demanding Baptist atmosphere, and had been handed every advantage and luxury without ever having had to work for any of it.

Also much like Senator Wheeler, Smith had developed some sort of a delusion wherein he seemed to think that he was specially chosen by God to help straighten out the evils of the world. Perhaps by some sort of divine intuition, he knew that part of his life's work seemed to be to guide others and to show them "the way".

Politically, he had been a faithful member of the Republican Party as far back as anyone could remember. He had been a member of the cabinet or worked in one way or another for every Republican President of the last thirty years.

He had always agreed with the Republican Party's philosophy and its goals, but as the years wore on, he became more impatient to accomplish his work and doing things the normal way seemed to be taking much too long.

When the N.N.P.P. was established he first of all noticed the flight of conservatives from both other parties. Because most members of this new party seemed more compatible with his thinking, he recognized it as a new and potentially potent ally. As soon as Tower announced that he intended to be its candidate and revealed some of his goals, Smith was quick to join.

Dick Smith was probably sincere in his goals and aspirations, but at the same time, he was somewhat self-delusional and zealous. He had such a narrow focus on the world that in most cases, objectivity was difficult if not impossible. It was as though he were looking at events through a telescope when he should have simply been using his unaided eyesight.

He was unmarried and it was unknown as to whether this was by design or circumstance. Nevertheless, since most of his time and much of his life was dedicated to his religious and political aims, he had no time left over for romance and professed very little interest in getting involved in a family.

All of these circumstances produced a rather impatient, unsympathetic, judgmental and somewhat nervous individual. Perhaps his occasional fear of a heart attack was psychologically understandable.

Glancing back over his shoulder as he noiselessly slipped in the door and closed it without a sound was Colonel Samuel Carter who now joined Dick Smith. Colonel Carter was the director of the Federal Investigative Agency.

In his earlier days, he had not been so fortunate as Dick Smith. He came from a broken home in the inner city of New York and as a child was not only neglected, but pushed around by almost everyone. As he grew older he was scared of everything and had no confidence in himself.

Eventually he ran into several members of a gang and was coerced into joining. They quickly taught him how to push back when threatened and soon he was the one initiating the threats. He found that security in numbers and the feeling of belonging was quite appealing. It also gave him his first inkling of the fact that there were two definite groups of people in the world. You either belonged to the controllers or you were the controlled. Naturally, he preferred the power of the former. Whether or not he realized it, it also helped to cover up any insecurities that still lay buried deep down inside of him.

At eighteen he joined the Army. He really had little choice as he was just one jump ahead of the law and it did keep him out of jail. At the same time, being part of the service and carrying weapons reinforced the previous taste of power and he found that he liked it—a lot! Soon thereafter and up until the present, Colonel Carter's consuming drive was to achieve more power—a need that never seemed to be satiated.

He worked his way through the ranks often at the expense of others. He went to Officers' Candidate School, got his second lieutenant's bars, bribed, threatened, cajoled, and kissed ass to make his way up towards the top.

By the time he had become a lieutenant colonel, he had long ago decided to court the Republican Party and its administrations. Even though not a brilliant person, he could figure out that the Republicans supported big defense budgets and military might, and that his power depended upon them.

When the C.I.A. and F.B.I. were combined into the Federal Investigative Agency he was known not only to Senator Wheeler and Dick Smith, but to several other members of Congress.

When the President was advised as to who should head the new organization, Carter's name was suggested and entered and he was appointed director. Of course he was on temporary duty from the Army as he had every intention of returning and continuing his rise in rank always keeping the position of General of the Army in his sights.

He had a wife and one son. Both of these he seldom saw. His wife, Nancy, was there for sex although that was something he rarely even thought about. She was also handy for publicity if he needed an escort to some ceremony or if the photographers were taking pictures on a particular day.

His son had even less importance. He had been sent to military academies most of his life. Contrary to his father's wishes, he decided not to follow a military career and instead found an interest in the theatre. From that day on, Colonel Carter practically disowned him and cut his very occasional contacts with him to none at all.

Sean Thompson, Tower's lawyer was the next to enter the little room. Unlike the other two already in the room, he never made any pretense at being driven by some noble cause either religious or political.

He had had only one main goal in life and that was to look out for number one and one strong motivation which was to make money, and if possible, at the expense of others. He was the closest thing to a total sociopath of anyone who had yet arrived.

He did have one intellectual pursuit and that was to use any law, no matter how obscure, to cover himself legally while performing any number of immoral acts. These included defending anyone who would pay the right price, and supporting anyone who would, in the end, be of benefit to him.

He was the perfect person to head a whole corps of similarly disposed lawyers who all worked for Tower.

"Has Tower been notified?" asked Dick Smith.

"Of course. He should be here any minute,"

responded Thompson.

As if on cue, Tower entered and sat down saying, "Let's get going gentlemen. I haven't much time."

Before answering, Dick Smith went over and locked the door. "Well, first of all Marshall, I for one, am worried about how far the President will let us go with our plans. He does support you, but he has no idea of the lengths to which we have gone without bringing him along."

"That is a problem, perhaps," answered Tower. "I am sure we can come up with some way either to convince him or to keep him totally out of the loop."

Sam Carter gave a hearty laugh and a couple of snorts.

"What is so funny?" demanded Smith.

"Fuckin' ironic! God damn! I have the simplest answer in the world for you mother fuckers!" boomed Carter.

"Colonel, please! Watch your language!" exclaimed Smith visibly shocked.

"Sorry Dickie Boy! Forgot where the f . . . er . . . hell I was. What is so f . . . d . . . er . . . darned funny is that I interviewed the President's personal physician and have I got news for you!"

"Well out with it," commanded Tower frustration audible in his tone of voice.

"Dr. What's-his-face told me in the strictest confidence that the poor bastard has had Alzheimer's disease for several years now and that soon he won't even know what is going on! How's that?"

"That would certainly work to our advantage providing that it can be kept secret," volunteered Smith. "How can we be sure that his doctor will keep it quiet?"

"We had the fu . . . er . . . little man checked out. Seems he is and has always been so damn loyal to the President that he would do anything for him. It's not political, mind you! Far from it. In fact, he has no interest at all in politics, but simply has a thing for the

President."

"I beg your pardon?" queried Tower somewhat taken aback.

"Oh, no. Shit. I did not mean it that way. He admires the man and is totally loyal to him and would never do anything that would harm him in any way. You see, he has been his personal physician ever since the President first ran for office. He is rather ancient and half senile himself now. He is so darned set in his ways that nothing would ever make him change his loyalties."

"Well I'll be damned," exclaimed Thompson.

"Please, watch your language! It is offensive!" interrupted Smith.

"Sorry old boy. Forgot how proper we are!" he added sarcastically. "I was about to say that I was beginning to suspect something was wrong lately with the President's few appearances in public. A lot of what he says doesn't seem to either make sense or ring absolutely true. At times he seemed as though he were just repeating memorized lines. I guess his advisers and White House staff must really be managing him."

"Yes. I was wondering what was going on myself," added Smith.

"Do they know what is wrong with him?" asked Tower.

"Hell no! His wife, what's-his-name the doctor, myself, and now you guys are the only people who know," responded Colonel Carter.

"Good! Let's keep it that way as long as possible and hopefully until Tower, here, is elected," added Smith.

"By the way, aren't there any problems with members of his staff or his cabinet should they find out what we are doing?" Tower wanted to know.

"We have nothing to worry about as long as we can get the President to agree and sign off on stuff. I can get him to sign anything even when he no longer really knows what it is. Even these days he seldom reads what he signs. Basically, he has always supported Tower. We've known that has been his position when he was a little more clear-headed and so does the staff and the cabinet. They should not be surprised if it should appear as though he is taking action to support our candidate. He and they do not need to know any of the details. As you know, I have always had direct and complete access to the President so no one would question or stop me," Smith finally stopped to take a breath.

Colonel Carter turning to Tower asked, "How's the electronic business doing?" and he winked.

"Couldn't be better! The company is making a lot of money," and he winked back.

Dick Smith, addressing himself to Thompson and Carter asked, "How is 5200 working out?"

"Just like clockwork! Those poor bastards didn't even know there was a secret appendix listing the criminal penalty phase of the bill. It was such a panic and rush job, their staffs never even asked for it. Besides, from what I hear, Senator Wheeler purposely limited the copies and most of the information given that day was through speeches. I doubt that very many members of the House know about the criminal specifications to this date. I'll bet my ass, though, that some are wishing they had known about it."

"What about Senator Butler? Have you decided to go after him yet?" Tower wanted to know.

"Hell, man. Don't get greedy. We have to leave a few members of the opposition around or it will look too damn obvious! Don't worry. If he causes too much trouble we'll go after him too," Carter drawled back. "We've knocked out enough of the opposition to practically insure your election already. With the upcoming Senatorial Election, the N.N.P.P. should have a majority for the first time. That should just about sew up passing anything you want."

"Yea and since we've got certain, shall we say, damaging evidence against several members of the F.C.C., we are guaranteed positive and glowing coverage on all the media from now until election day for the House and later the Presidency," beamed Thomspon.

"Good work men! I won't forget this when I am elected," offered Tower.

Each person left the room, one at a time, and each in turn thought briefly about his future.

"You bet your ass, you won't!" commented Colonel Samuel Carter who was first to leave, and who already had visions of becoming a full general knowing that the President is still and will be the Commander in Chief of all the armed forces.

Dick Smith, second to leave, thought about a possible Vice-Presidential position. Tower hadn't mentioned any choices, let alone announced his running mate. "After all," Smith thought, "I have worked in government all my life. I am the perfect choice. Must bring this up to him next chance I get. As Vice-President, as leader of the N.N.P.P., and as tie breaker in the New Combined House, I'd be in a perfect position to see that this country sticks to the laws and that people behave as they should!"

Sean Thompson slipped out next into the night air thinking, "I can think of three positions that would work to my advantage. As secretary of the treasury, not only would my salary be increased many fold, but I would be in a position to make lots more money from inside information not yet known to the public."

He paused for a second and then went on dreaming, "Better yet, as chairman of the Federal Reserve Board, I would help set interest rates and could make a mint from advanced knowledge of economic conditions! Talk about your inside traders!"

Again, he stopped to take a deep breath and then continued thinking, "If neither of those pan out, I wouldn't mind getting the nomination for Attorney General. I'd be right in my field of expertise and could benefit from it just as I always have except, of course, on a much grander scale."

As Tower turned off the light and closed the door, he

at first wondered what it would take, to not only repay these men for their help in getting him elected, but what it would cost to keep them forever silent!

He let it slide for the moment more concerned with the feeling that the Presidency was within his grasp. He couldn't wait for the inauguration. At the thought of millions of people all over the world, with their admiring eyes on him and his name on their adoring lips, he suddenly became terribly and irreversibly sexually excited!

Chapter VI

SUSPICIONS

The sun shone ruby-red through the pollution hanging heavily midway between sky and earth on a hot Washington afternoon in August. Senator Butler, deep in thought, sat at a desk in his office, both hands supporting his chin.

He couldn't help but notice the absences in the Combined House. At each session, fewer senators seemed in attendance and most of the absences seemed to be from his own party. He was particularly curious about Senator Morton who never returned from the weekend break and Senator Owens who vanished in the middle of a session.

"It just can't all be a massive coincidence!" he murmured to himself. "I've got to find out what is going on. After all, people aren't absent for several weeks without some explanation." He had heard nothing in the electronic media, and no one he had talked to seemed to have the slightest clue as to their whereabouts.

He knew that Senator Morton was not married, and since he knew nothing about his family, he could not contact them. He had met Senator Owen's wife, but she was back in Ohio.

"I know. I'll pay a personal visit to Johnson's wife and see if she knows anything," he thought. He did know that Mrs. Larry Johnson lived in Washington most of the year.

Butler drove his own commuter vehicle to the Johnson's house. As he pulled up he noticed that the grounds were surrounded by a high black wrought iron fence, and that there was a security gate. The old victorian style house appeared very large and looked as though it could accommodate a good sized Washington party.

"I'd sure be curious to know some of the history behind this place," he murmured as he left the vehicle and pressed a manual button at the gate.

"Obviously, all authorized personnel were able to use a video-lazer and didn't have to leave their vehicles," he thought with some irritation. A video camera panned slowly and focused on him. A mechanical sounding voice droned, "State your business and identify yourself!"

He did as he was told and added that he wished to speak to Mrs. Johnson.

"What is the nature of your business?" repeated the voice.

"I am afraid that that is confidential. Mrs. Johnson knows who I am. I am sure she will see me," he added.

After a couple of minutes, the gate clicked open and silently slid back on hidden rails. He ran back to his commuter and drove on in and up the horseshoe drive stopping before the front portico.

As he climbed the stairs, the door was already open and a servant in uniform ushered him into a small vestibule right off the front hallway. The man left him saying, "Mrs. Johnson will be right with you."

As he waited, Butler thought back at the few occasions he had seen her and tried to remember what she looked like, "As I recall, she was rather attractive, a little on the plump side, somewhere in her fifties with blondish hair, and sort of bubbly and effervescent in demeanor." He also had the impression that she was always impeccably groomed with not a hair out of place and that she had a rather outgoing personality.

He was suddenly startled out of his thoughts by a voice right behind him saying, "Senator Butler. What can I do for you?"

As Butler turned around to answer he was momentarily shocked into silence. The woman standing before him was not at all as he had remembered Mrs.

Johnson. This woman was much thinner, almost to the point of being haggard. Her hair was white and disheveled. She was wearing a housecoat and slippers and had on no make-up. She looked as though she hadn't slept nor eaten for days. Dark circles accented her tired eyes. Her hand trembled visibly as she tended it to Butler.

As he took her hand, he was aware that it was as cold as ice. For a moment he really wasn't sure that this was Mrs. Johnson, the senator's wife.

Haltingly he asked, "Mrs. Johnson? Are you all right?"

"As a matter of fact I have not been feeling too well, but let's talk about you. What is it that you want?"

"Mrs. Johnson, are you aware that your husband has not been present at the House for some time now? I thought that you might tell me where he is or what has happened to him. Has he been sick too?"

"Well he hasn't been feeling too well lately either," she responded weakly, avoiding his eyes.

"Could I please speak to him for a moment?" he wanted to know.

"I'm afraid that is out of the question. He isn't here."

"Where is he then? Did he go to a medical center?"

"Please, you must go! I really don't want to talk about it," she answered with unmistakable fear in her eyes as she looked over her shoulder as though she expected someone to be there.

"Sure I'll go especially if it upsets you, but can't you just tell me where your husband is?"

"He, he, has been . . . er . . ." and she stopped.

"Yes? He has been what?" Butler wanted to know.

"He has been arrested!" she whispered. "Now go! Please!" and she quickly left the room.

Butler stood frozen, staring at the spot where she had been, until the servant stirred him back to consciousness and efficiently ushered him out of the room and out the front door.

As he got back into his commuter vehicle and slowly

drove off, he was absolutely baffled. "Arrested? For what? I didn't even have a chance to ask!"

As he drove back towards his office, he was more puzzled than ever. Sitting back down at his desk, he decided to try and find out where Senator Johnson was, and for what he had been was arrested. He activated the videophone, but because of some sort of intuition, he shut off the video part so that no one could see who was calling although he could still see who was on the other end.

He punched in the code for the People's Protective Police Headquarters.

A female officer in uniform appeared on the screen, "This is P.P.P. Headquarters. How may I help you? Incidentally, your video is off!"

"Sorry about that. There seems to be something wrong with it. I've called Repair Central and they should get to it soon," he hoped the ruse worked. "I am trying to find the whereabouts of Senator Larry Johnson. Someone told me that he has been arrested."

"I see by your number that you are calling from Capitol Hill. Is this official business?" she wanted to know.

"Well, yes and no," he answered. "I am calling from a House office and have noticed that Senator Johnson has been gone for quite a while."

"Well, if as you say, he has really been arrested, he probably is stored in Regional Rehabilitation Plant Number One."

"Well, how do I find out? When is his court date? Of what is he being accused?" he blurted out while also momentarily wrestling with the use of the word "stored". He hadn't heard it officially used before, but quickly dismissed it as perhaps a synonym for "jailed" and nothing more.

"Sorry, but I am not authorized to give out that information. If he was arrested under CHB 5200, his trial will be handled in Internal Court which is not open to the public."

"CHB 5200? What are you talking about? There was no penalty or criminal part of that bill! Internal Court? Listen sister, are you sure you haven't lost some of your marbles?"

"What is your name, Sir?" she demanded with a certain threatening tone that he recognized.

He quickly hung up hoping she wouldn't bother tracing the call all the way to his office.

"Stupid! I should have used someone else's videophone or a public one," he chastised himself.

"Son-of-a-bitch! Can CHB 5200 actually have a criminal section? I never saw one! That doesn't make any sense, unless of course, they have some way of getting people to admit to things they wouldn't otherwise talk about! Christ! That probably means drugs or torture of some sort!"

"But how do they even find out that there is any potential for violation of the law? Could it include anyone who disagrees with the N.N.P.P.'s agenda? Did they go that far? If so, as long as one kept quiet about certain things one ought to be relatively safe. Maybe that's it. Maybe Johnson's, Owens', and Morton's speeches opposing N.N.P.P.'s bills was all it took! If that's the case, though, I would have been the first to go! I've been fighting their bills right along with the rest of them."

"All I know is that this country is in deep trouble! I wondered what Wheeler had up his sleeve, but the bill was so ridiculous that I thought no one would really take it seriously. Thought maybe they were just humoring an old temperamental man! Shit was I wrong!" he concluded and stared for a while in stunned silence.

He slowly let the full impact of the implications of the last few hours sweep over him. As it did so, he broke out in a cold sweat and was aware of the loud pounding of his heart in his ears. He recognized these symptoms as a slowly invading, and massively paralyzing fear. He felt faint and then absolutely powerless.

Something had been swimming around in his mind, just below the surface, for some time now, as it sometimes does just prior to full wakefulness after a night's sleep. It had been nagging at him ever since the fight with Wheeler over the CHB 5200 floor fight, but he had not quite put the events together until now.

"Idiot! Moron! How could I be so stupid?" he thought again as it hit him. "I've been so busy fighting individual bills that I lost sight of the broader picture! So did we all! Maybe that was the plan? Keep us off center until it was too late?"

He grasped the edge of his desk with both hands until the blood drained out of them and they became numb. After a few moments, he half arose from his chair and then plopped back down again talking to the walls as there was no one else present at the time, "Christ! If you take the present Supreme Court make-up, add to it the majority the N.N.P.P. now has from the last mid-term election, the possible hidden part of CHB 5200, and Tower announcing and then nominated for President as the N.N.P.P.'s candidate, it all adds up to conspiracy with a capital C! It has happened several times before, but never on this scale! What is worse, it has gone so far this time, that I doubt it can be stopped!"

As often happens in cases of threat or self-preservation, fear, which at first paralyzes, often turns into a motivation for action. In Senator Butler's case, the adrenalin began to flow as his mind spun with ideas that he could hardly sort out.

"Gotta think! Considering what's happened to several other key members of my party, I must be in immense danger of receiving a similar fate. Still puzzled as to why I am still free! What about the kids and Elizabeth? Also her mother? The way Mrs. Johnson looked scared out of ten years of her life, they must have pressured or threatened her or even worse. Can't take that chance with my family! Got to get them out of Washington. No, better yet, out of the country and hopefully one with no extradition treaty with the U.S."

He jumped out of his chair so abruptly that it tipped over and went clattering across the marbled floor. The echo of the noise from the chair suddenly shocked him back to the realization that it was imperative to control himself and pretend that all was normal. "It is Friday afternoon. I'll just tell my staff I'm taking off early for the weekend. Yea, that's it."

He opened the door of his staff's office and, smiling, yelled across the room to his executive secretary, "Say Mary, would you cancel my appointments for the afternoon and reschedule?"

"Why of course Senator. Anything wrong?"

"Thanks. No, nothing wrong. I am a little tired and want to get an early start on the week-end. Also, I am seeing Elizabeth and the kids off on a little vacation. Have a nice weekend. See you Monday."

"Thank you Senator. You too."

He closed the door, activated the videophone intending to call his wife. On second thought he decided to avoid using videophones altogether, especially his, and shut it off.

He reached down and grabbed his coat off the back of the fallen chair and put it on. He then picked the chair back off the floor and replaced it at his desk.

For a minute he thought of checking his computer crystals to see if there was anything on them that he could use as evidence. House business and records could be accessed from anyone's computer, and anything used was usually stored on that office's crystals.

If there was he could take them with him, but he speculated, "I'll have to get to that later. I'd have to go back and ask Mary and that would be bound to raise suspicions. Better just head on home and get Elizabeth on her way."

He forced himself to walk as slowly and normally as possible to the House commuter vehicle storage area. On his way he passed Senator Wheeler who stiffly nodded at him. He forced himself to return the gesture adding a tiny polite smile.

"I wonder if he knows what he has gotten us all into?" he asked himself as he started the commuter and drove off into the Friday afternoon gridlock.

Chapter VII

SAFEGUARDING

As he dodged traffic on his way home, Butler tried to solidify some sort of a plan. Once he got on the throughway, he programmed the commuter vehicle and it went on automatic. This gave him some time to think.

"I'd better not even tell Elizabeth anything precise," he thought. "I'll just try to let her know that it is urgent to convince the rest that they are taking a little vacation and explain everything when, or if, I can join up with them later. I'd better get them to the air shuttleport as soon as I can make reservations. Can't do that! That would be too dangerous. Must use a travel vehicle. That's it! We'll rent one. Less security."

Although he fully trusted Elizabeth's ability to keep everything confidential, and her strength to act calmly under stress, he felt it was safer for her not to know the specifics of his suspicions at this point.

He had met Elizabeth Butler, then Elizabeth Browning, during his first campaign for the Senate. She did not have to work having come from well-to-do parents who lived in West Palm Beach. She was simply filling in time helping out in the campaign while she decided what to do with her life. They had been immediately attracted in every way to each other, and as soon as he won his seat they were married.

They had two children. First to arrive was Michael who attended Junior Technology School and later they had Judy who was in Primary Preparatory School. He hoped that they would be home.

He had to worry as well about Elizabeth's mother. She had moved in with them two years ago when her husband died. Both Elizabeth and he had insisted upon it. She tended to be very independent, and often either forgot to inform anyone of her whereabouts or ended up going somewhere she hadn't planned.

The beeper sounded, and the red light flashed on the console indicating that the vehicle was nearing the exit. Soon Butler would have to retake control working his way through surface streets. In the meantime, he thought about his own course of action.

"First of all, I had better return to work Monday and continue as much as possible with the regular routine. Summer recess is coming up in less than two weeks. At that time I could get away and rejoin the family if I feel it is necessary. Too precipitous a departure would attract too much attention. Better to attempt to make it appear as a planned vacation. Besides, I want to make an attempt, even if futile, to stop this 'thing'!"

As he exited the commuter vehicle and entered the house, he first ran into Alice. She was supposed to be the housekeeper, but had been employed since the birth of Michael and was more like part of the family.

"Hello Alice," he said casually.

"Why hello Richard. What are you doing home so early?" she asked with mild curiosity tinging her voice.

"Oh, I decided to take off a little early. Are mother, Elizabeth and the kids home yet?"

"Sure. Elizabeth has been here all afternoon working in her office. Michael just got back and Judy's in her room."

"What about Mrs. Browning?" Butler wanted to know.

Alice gave a little chuckle, "She managed not to get lost today. She's in watching the videoscreen. Anything wrong?" She peered at him with the experienced eyes of one who knows someone well—perhaps too well.

"No. Nothing wrong. Elizabeth, mother and the kids were thinking of taking a little vacation and I am about to set the plans. Feel like going with them on a little trip?"

"Where to? I haven't heard anyone talk about it. Who would be here to take care of you?"

"Well, I'll probably join all of you as soon as recess starts. As soon as we've got it all settled, we'll let you know. In the meantime, I take it I can plan on including you?"

"Sure if you feel I'm needed and if it isn't somewhere too primitive for this old body."

"Don't worry it won't be," and with that Butler was off to talk to his wife.

Before he got there he suddenly thought about the house being under surveillance and possibly filled with electronic eavesdropping devices.

"I had better use a pen and paper just to be safe," he thought.

He mounted the main staircase and headed for a small room next to the main bedroom which Elizabeth used as her office. (In addition to running the house, she did enough charity work and political lobbying to keep her well-occupied.) It was crammed with files, letters, papers, a computer, a videophone, a fairly large desk, and a videoscreen which was recessed into the wall. All of these gave the room an atmosphere of regulated confusion.

As he entered, he found her busily scrutinizing a long list of names. Her viewing aids were slightly askew which somewhat detracted from her serious countenance.

He bent over her and, with pretended routine, kissed her perfunctorily on the cheek saying, "Hello dear. How was your day?"

"Oh, hi honey. Fine. What are you doing home?" she wanted to know.

"Well, glad to see you too," he tried to keep his voice calm.

He picked up one of her many pads of paper and a pen and wrote, "Don't say a word! Come with me into the hygieneum. I'll explain. Act normal."

"Wh . . .?" she started to say, but he gently put his hand over her mouth.

He led her by the hand and through the master bedroom into the hygieneum. Once there he turned on the vacupump, the whirlpool, the sprinkler, and anything else that would make noise.

"What's this all about?" she demanded to know.

Making a sign to be quiet he said, "Let's clean-up together, honey. I'm feeling romantic," and wrote, "I think the house is under surveillance, but I do not know the method, so I'm taking no chances. I must write everything down, but out loud pretend all is normal. Shake your head if you understand."

She shook her head then said, "Well, honey, if you really want us to do it together, I'm game. We haven't done that for a long time."

"Right dear. Let's take off our clothes," he replied then wrote, "Slowly!"

He continued, "Dangerous situation has arisen. Will explain details later. Must get you, kids, and your mother out of country just to be safe. Want you to tell them and Alice that you are going on a vacation and that I'll join later. Must head for Canada. Shuttling too dangerous. We'll rent travel vehicle. Understand?"

"Sure, Richard. It will be fun!" she replied shaking her head again indicating that she understood the double meaning.

"As soon as finished here, take rest of family out back by pool. Explain quietly. Gather them near the filter pump. Convince them you are taking them on real vacation. Tell them Vancouver. Act normal!"

Elizabeth looked anything but normal for a minute. In fact she looked terrified as anyone would under the circumstances.

She took a deep breath, put her blouse back on and buttoned it, straightened her hair and make-up in the mirror—something that always made her feel better anyway, stared for a second at Richard, gave him a long and sincere kiss, and turned and exited the room.

He stared at the back of his departing wife. Although he believed that no one could possibly have heard anything with all the gadgets going, he hoped that they nevertheless spent enough time to fool someone into believing that they could have been making love.

He turned off all the appliances and then headed downstairs to his office. It was large and imposing compared to hers and it contained his business computer.

"Let's see now. Must transfer some money, but not enough to raise suspicions, to Mail Center, Vancouver. Must use Express Foreign Exchange Draft. They'll reserve hotel when they get there. Need a copy of Passport and Social Security files for each one. I guess that will cover it for the time being," he thought as he started to manually punch information into his computer having abandoned the notion of using the dictation mode.

He hoped that the transfer of money wouldn't raise alarms. He knew that obtaining passport and Social Security files caused routine recordings in each citizen's Life Transaction dossier. Yet, he hoped that the destination of Vancouver might be ordinary enough not to cause the files to be flagged for further action.

Having printed the necessary documents, he gathered them, put them in a plain Manila envelope, and went back upstairs to join his wife.

While working on his computer he had heard voices and the sound of stampeding feet which told him the rest were already up there packing.

"From the enthusiastic noises sounds like they not only bought the idea, but liked it as well. Elizabeth must have put on a great performance. Perhaps she missed her calling!" he added semi-seriously.

"Here Liz. Put this in a safe place." He showed her the contents of the envelope prior to sealing it, pointing specifically to the Vancouver Mail Center destination of the money draft.

"Thanks dear. I am sure we will have an enjoyable

time. I'm really looking forward to this vacation." She added the last a little louder than the rest so that if anyone were listening, they would not miss that part.

"I am sure you deserve it," he replied with a slight nod of his head. "I'll take this and the other travel kits and put them in the tandem. I'll see you down there."

He waited impatiently in the commuter vehicle shelter. His inner tension was revealed by the nervous and unconscious tapping of his foot.

The silence was quickly broken by excited voices as the group entered.

"Which shuttle are we taking dad?" Michael wanted to know.

"Sorry, kids. You will be going by travel vehicle this time," he replied watching the excited looks on their young faces disappear.

"Aw, I wanted to fly," volunteered Judy with a trembling of her lower lip which indicated that not only was she disappointed, but that she was close to tears.

Richard took her in his arms, gave her a warm and secure hug, caressed her hair, gave her a peck on the forehead, and with great difficulty released her saying, "I know how you feel dear. It is necessary this one time. You can take the shuttle when you come back home. Okay honey?"

"Okay dad," she answered looking somewhat cheered.

"That's my girl," he replied having trouble controlling his own tears.

Judy, puzzled, looked at him carefully, and although she was too young to really figure anything out, her instinct told her that her dad was feeling something out of the ordinary. Her mind was like the lens of a camera that was almost, but not quite, focused.

"Let's get going," he tried to sound authoritative.

"Are we all going to be able to fit in?" Alice wanted to know.

"It will be a little crowded for now, but when we switch to the travel vehicle, we will have plenty of space," Elizabeth explained.

He started the commuter vehicle, pulled out onto the street, drove to the nearest on-ramp of the throughway, programmed the commuter for a rental station as far removed from the center of town as possible, and they were on their way.

The red light blinked and the beeper sounded as he took over the controls of the vehicle and drove off the throughway.

They were in a section far from the center of town in which none of them had ever been before. There were a few stores and buildings in use, but most seemed closed and rather dingy and run-down as well.

On his right Butler noticed a long fence which seemed to have no end. When he read the sign indicating that it was a "restricted area" and saw a few people milling around in the late afternoon dusk, he realized it was one of those "ghettos for the homeless" he had heard about.

From the brief descriptions he had read about or heard, he never imagined the depths of deprivation that really existed. Apparently, in polite society and official circles, it was gauche to speak about such conditions. "Perhaps it is even dangerous," he thought.

"Where in the blessed world are we going Richard?" Alice wanted to know with obvious anxiety registering in her voice. "Do you intend to get us all lost or worse killed? Look at this place! Nothing but bums over there!"

"Yea, Dad. Why are we in this neighborhood?" Michael chimed in.

Butler thought rapidly and then answered, "Sorry guys, but this probably was the most convenient area to rent a vehicle. That's where the computer sent us. Maybe they have more available. Anyway, once we enter the vehicle storage rental area, we will be perfectly safe!"

Elizabeth kept quiet.

After a few more detours heading away from the restricted area, they came upon the rental storage area.

Richard pulled up inside a massive building filled with every conceivable type of vehicle from commuters and transporters to tandems and very large vans.

He stopped in front of a sign which read, "Renters' Parking Area" and got out.

"All right folks. You stay here and I'll be as quick as I can. Elizabeth, I need the envelope. Thank you," and he walked towards another sign that said, "Vehicle Rentals—this way".

He followed a yellow line which eventually led him to a large compound filled with people, counters, computers and clerks.

He walked up to one of the counters which stood below yet another sign which read, "For Destinations Out of Country—North America."

"Can I help you, Sir?" asked a sallow-looking young man who was wearing the agency's yellow uniform.

"Why yes. I'd like to rent a travel vehicle."

"For yourself?" asked the clerk in a routine, almost bored manner.

"Why no. It's for my family and our housekeeper."

"What is your destination and how long will you be needing it?"

"They are going to Canada, er . . . to Vancouver to start. I'm not sure how long exactly. It partly depends on when I can get away and join them," answered Butler feeling rather nervous and slightly impatient at all the questions being asked.

"Fine and how many in the party at present?" asked the clerk.

"Altogether four people. I am not sure whether we will be needing it for the return trip or whether we'll use the air shuttle," he added.

"Well if you will step this way, sir," said the clerk as he headed to a desk where there was a computer terminal. "I'll need to see Social Security papers on all going now. Also, what is the purpose of your trip?"

Butler handed over the envelope containing the

required papers, but kept the duplicate of the money draft and slipped it into his pocket deciding that he would mail it at the nearest mail center as soon as they were safely off. "We, well actually they, are going on a little vacation, and as I said before, I hope to join them for part of it." With great difficulty, he struggled to quell the urge of adding several sarcastic remarks that came to mind.

"I see you have your Passport files up to date. Shall I charge this to your Washington bank?"

"Uh? Oh, no. My wife has an account for such purposes. Charge it to hers. Her name is Elizabeth. Elizabeth Butler."

As he had foreseen, each time a Social Security file is used for any purpose, it is noted on that person's record. He had overlooked the fact that he needed to pay for the rental of the vehicle in advance and that the cost had to be charged to an account. "Should be considered routine and not anything very unusual, I hope."

Business concluded, Butler retraced his steps along the yellow line and rejoined his family.

Soon a travel vehicle pulled up. The travel kits were transferred to the rear storage of the vehicle. A tandem was not needed as this was a much larger vehicle which had internal storage. It was safer, and provided greater security, especially considering the fact that the vehicle could reach speeds of one hundred fifty miles per hour when on automatic.

With a few tears, and many hugs and kisses, they exchanged good-byes. "Have a safe trip and a good time," Butler yelled at the departing vehicle.

With heavy heart and fighting back tears that were very close to surfacing he kept watching as the vehicle slowly pulled out into the inky blackness of the night. He sadly wondered if he would ever see his loved ones again.

Chapter VIII

REHABILITATION

The loud clickings of multiple heels echoed through one of the wings of Regional Rehabilitation Plant Number Three. Two orderlies dressed in white lab coats, and one doctor dressed in a yellow coat, paused before the first blinking green light.

"Amanda Simpson . . ." read one of the orderlies looking at an almost invisible minicomputer screen set into the white wall of the endless hallway at eye level. "Time to wake up, honey," he added.

The other orderly read from the next computer screen near which an equally brilliant green light blinked. It was accompanied by the noise of a steady buzzer. "Huh! George Simpson. Must be that broad's husband. Boy they must be horny after all this time. Don't you think so Phil?"

Phil nodded and then added, "I sure would be if I had been stored that long."

"Can you imagine going over four years without any?" Joe inquired.

"Even you would look good to me after that time," Phil kidded.

"Gentlemen! Boys! May I remind you that we have a serious job to do!" interrupted Doctor Richardson. "And you Phil, I wouldn't even joke about that! You know how many homosexuals are here just for thinking what you just said!" He stared intently at Phil trying to decipher whether or not the remark was really meant in jest.

Phil, looking alarmed, answered, "You know I was just joking doctor. Just habit you know. Sorry."

"All right, but watch it. You young ones have a

tendency to forget the law!" Dr. Richardson pressed a button recessed into the wall, and a heretofore invisible door moved up into the ceiling with a whooshing sound.

Inside the small cubicle was a coffin-sized plastic tube suspended half way between floor and ceiling and held there with almost invisible wires. The tube itself contained the seemingly lifeless body of George Simpson which appeared to be surrounded by a clear, jello-like substance. Electrodes were attached at various parts of the body and three tubes were also connected. One of these entered the nose. One came from a catheter attached to the urinary tract, and the third was attached somewhere in the area of the jugular vein.

The walls of the small room were filled with electronic equipment including one major computer console. All the wires and tubes attached to the body were connected in turn to various machines on the walls.

"According to the chart, boys, it is time to start this man's rehabilitation programming," stated Dr. Richardson in a business-like manner.

"What about Amanda Simpson?" Phil inquired.

"We'll get to her next. We only have six hands," replied the doctor.

"Yea, sure right," answered Phil wondering in turn if the doctor was being serious. "Wasn't funny anyway," he thought. "He's such a dumb shit!"

"First we'll give him the usual massive dose of drugs to remove past memory," commanded Richardson. "Get the electro-encephalograph ready. After the administration of drugs, I'll program the computer to bring him almost to consciousness. Then we'll check to be sure that he has no memory of past events."

Dr. Richardson removed a small black leather case from an inside pocket of his lab coat. He opened the case and took out a crystal containing the computer codes for the routine rehabilitation drug program and inserted it into the computer. Then the computer automatically commanded that certain drugs, stored in dispensing machines, be fed into the correct tubes.

During this time, the body that was George Simpson showed the first signs of life by changing expressions rapidly and violently. After about five minutes, an electronic bell rang.

"The drug program is complete, boys. Now, we are ready to see if it worked completely."

"No shit! We've done this a thousand times and he acts like we just arrived!" thought Joe to himself.

Richardson removed another crystal from the leather case. He exchanged it for the one already in the computer saying, "Now this program will bring him to just the right state of consciousness to allow us to test his memory without awakening him."

Again the computer went to work and color returned to the body. Involuntary muscle twitches could be observed. The eyes fluttered and sounds in the form of deep moans could be heard even through the closed tube. Shallow, intermittent breathing began.

"Time to drain enough of the life support fluids to allow him to breathe on his own and to open the top of the storage tube," the doctor commanded.

"Yes Sir," answered Phil, but was really thinking, "Thanks Dr. Frankenstein. I didn't know that!" He nevertheless proceeded to do as told.

"Now, Joe you monitor the electro-encephalogram while I initiate the usual series of questions. Phil, you watch the cardiac oscilloscope carefully. Make sure that it stays within parameters," barked the doctor.

Joe and Phil simply glanced at each other with expressions of exaggerated and mocking exasperation and then followed orders.

For a few minutes the computer transmitted questions concerning Simpson's past to certain receiving electrodes. Joe kept his eyes on a mostly blank computer printout. Finally, Dr. Richardson turned to him and asked, "Do we have a good encephalograph?"

"Yes, doctor. Looks normal judging from all the

rehabs I've seen."

"Nevertheless, feed it into the reader just to be absolutely sure," replied the doctor.

This Joe proceeded to do as Richardson carefully peered at the computer screen. Nothing appeared on the screen except a massive array of row upon rows of the digit "1" constantly flickering across the screen from top to bottom.

"Success! He has absolutely no memory of his past! Phil, signal the transition station for a monitor cart," Richardson ordered.

Phil walked over to one of the panels in the wall and pressed a button. In the meantime, Joe and the doctor were removing the tubes and electrodes and draining the rest of the fluids from the large storage container.

The three of them then proceeded to vacuum Simpson's body, and by the time they were through, a small cart-like vehicle, which floated on air in a manner similar to a hovercraft, noiselessly pulled up to the open door. Except for a seat and a control panel, the rest of the cart looked like a giant incubator. It was surrounded by clear glass or plastic and had places to insert arms and hands from the outside without breaking the airtight seals. In addition, it had electronic monitoring equipment and its share of tubes and electrodes.

The orderly who had driven up opened up one end of the incubator-like prism and proceeded to assist the other three in transferring George from the storage tube to the cart.

"Easy! Easy!" yelled Dr. Richardson.

"What's he think we are going to do? Drop him and break him into pieces?" thought Joe.

Turning to the driver of the cart, Dr. Richardson commanded in his apparently usual authoritative tone, "I want this rehabilitated person taken to the transition area. There you are to monitor him until you receive further instructions. Is that clear?"

The driver answered in the affirmative and then

drove off, a little faster and more recklessly than is normally allowed.

"I'll have to report that son-of-a-bitch! Did you guys get his I.D. badge number?" grumbled Richardson.

Both Joe and Phil shook their heads to signify that they hadn't.

"Doesn't matter. I'll find out anyway," he replied to no one in particular. He pressed the original button that had opened the door and it closed silently. "Don't forget to leave instructions to have this room readied for the next person."

"We won't," replied Phil.

They all walked down to the next cubicle. The doctor pressed its button and the door opened revealing Amanda Simpson's body suspended in the same manner as her husband's had been. Except for the different body, the scene was an exact duplicate of the last cubicle.

"Well my dear. You are about to join your husband. Unfortunately, you will not know that he is your husband," chuckled Dr. Richardson.

The same process was started on Amanda as had been on George. Some color came back to her flesh, and involuntary muscular contractions started to appear. Suddenly, though, her contorted face froze in position and the color drained back out of her skin. This happened at exactly the point where Dr. Richardson had started to initiate the series of questions about her past.

A loud warning bell rang. Richardson, paling noticeably, turned to Phil and asked in a controlled voice that betrayed just a slight bit of alarm, "What have you got, Phil?"

"Nothing! She's flatlined!"

"You Joe?"

"Absolutely flat encephalograph! No spikes, no nothing!"

Dr. Richardson rushed over to the computer and worked for a good five minutes. During that time the loud alarm bell continued to ring steadily. Finally, he said, "Shut that damn bell off! It's no use. She's dead!"

"What do we do now?" asked Phil

"Let me think for a minute. It's nothing we did. I followed the same routine that I have thousands of times before. I'll run an analytical check just to be sure."

"Do you want me to contact the judge? He can change the sentence to the death penalty and then no one will question anything. I've had him do that several times when we screwed up," Joe added.

"Well I didn't screw up as you put it so that won't be necessary! My guess is that her heart gave out and once I check for sure, that's the reason I'll write down on the certificate!"

"Yes doctor. I guess you know best!" remarked Phil.

"You're damn right about that! Now signal the Morgue Disposal Division and have them come and pick up this body. I'll run the check while we are waiting."

"Are you going to ask them to store her for further study or dispose of the remains?" Joe wanted to know.

Hesitating and thinking it over for a minute, Dr. Richardson finally made a decision. "Tell them to disintegrate and dispose of the body. That way no one will be able to dispute my findings, right?" and he winked.

Somewhat surprised, the two orderlies noticed the wink and thought that they understood its meaning. Since they weren't in the mood for what they considered rather sick humor, and especially considering the source, they decided to ignore it and proceed to do as told.

As an afterthought Joe mused to himself, "He probably just has a strange tic that only shows itself under stress!"

* * *

At about the same time, a maintenance tender was walking down another white corridor in another part of the country. This man was checking to see that all was in working order in Regional Rehabilitation Plant Number One, the Washington compound.

As he strolled nonchalantly, he would stop at each miniscreen to make sure that all systems were checking out and that there were no problems.

As this was an endless, monotonous and boring job, he amused himself by reading the names of the occupants out loud. He talked to them as though he knew them personally.

"Well, hello there Senator Owens! Sleeping well I see. Don't worry. Your time to wake up is coming up soon! Nice talking to you," he would add and then would stroll on to the next screen.

"What have we here? Another senator. Well, bless my soul. Aren't we privileged! Don't you worry either Fred Morton. Your time is coming up soon as I see from your screen. Should be blinking any month now." He walked still further and stopped in front of still another screen.

"My word! Another member of the House. This place is full of you guys. Just a little while longer for you too. Be patient!"

He kept on walking from one screen to another and finally, shaking his head, he turned around and spoke to the lot, "I must say fellows that this place really caters to high class people! Your Party must be missing you. Too bad you won't wake up in time for the upcoming election! By the time you are out, you'll really be out—of office too! Hope you eventually get to meet the new president before you move! The polls say that Tower is a shoo-in."

Thinking that some of what he had said might have struck his "customers" as funny, he laughed out loud at his own cleverness, and then proceeded down the hall continuing his endless boring routine.

Chapter IX

COUNTERING

After a couple of very restless and almost sleepless nights, Senator Butler was once again back in his House office. Having temporarily taken care of his family as best as he knew how, he was sill trying to formulate some sort of a plan of action.

"I suppose I'd better start by obtaining a copy of CHB 5200 and see what the penalty section involves. That way, I'll at least have an idea of what I'm up against," he thought. He buzzed Mary into his office.

"Good morning Senator. Have a nice weekend?" she asked.

"It was okay," he answered evasively. "Mary, could you please print out a coy of CHB 5200 for me? I'm particularly interested in any attachments to the bill. O.K.?"

"Certainly Senator. Right away," she called on her way back into her own office. She typed the code for the Congressional Record into her computer. She added CHB 5200 when queried. The printer spit out the bill in just a few seconds as it was only three pages long.

She thumbed through the papers looking for additions to the main bill. Finding none, she turned to the computer and retyped the code for CHB 5200 and then added a request for any appendices.

To her surprise the screen read, "ACCESS DENIED. Appendices A through D to CHB 5200 classified TOP SECRET. Only authorized 'Need to Know' personnel with special category clearance allowed to access."

Mary had never run across anything like this before. Only the minutes of closed sessions of Intelligence or

Military committees were ever classified and never bills passed in open session. Staring in total disbelief at what she had just read, and being at a momentary loss as to what to do next, she froze. After a couple of minutes she let out a breath of relief as an idea occurred to her.

"Must be an error," she thought. "Maybe I pushed the wrong key or something. Better try it again."

Each time she tried, the results were the same. Finally, she burst through Senator Butler's door startling him.

"What the hell, Mary! You scared me," he exclaimed.

"Sorry Richard, er, I mean Senator. Regarding CHB 5200, come take a look. I've never seen anything like it."

He followed her back to her office and stared at the screen. "I was afraid of that!" he mumbled after a couple of minutes.

"Since when don't we access to public records?" Mary wanted to know.

He feared that most probably the offices were bugged. Therefore he thought it would be better to both keep Mary in the dark as much as possible and not discuss any aspects of the situation in this part of the building. He replied, "Don't get upset. I'm sure it is an error. Probably a glitch in the accessing coder or something like that. I'll check into it. Thanks Mary."

Although at first puzzled, and then suspicious, she shrugged her shoulders and returned to her office closing the door, leaving the Senator deep in thought once more.

"Somehow, from everything I've seen and heard, everything seems to point to Tower. Of course he's had a lot of help all over the place, but my guess would be that he's in control or at least a main player. He has been a big supporter of Senator Wheeler both monetarily and verbally."

"He has a monopoly on government electronics. That may somehow be connected to all the surveillance. After all, he has unlimited technology at his fingertips and from everything I've heard, he wouldn't hesitate to use it. He's never been known to turn aside anything that might give him an advantage of any sort."

"He is the candidate for the New National People's Party and everything that has happened has worked to his benefit including, of course, the arrests of most of the opposition."

"He recently came out publicly in stating that he has always supported CHB 5200 and backs its precepts without reservations. Ha! That's a laugh! He probably invented the damn thing himself!"

"The media spits out one version of every news story. By some strange coincidence all of it is glowingly favorable to Tower! There can be little doubt about it. He has to be at the center! I just wonder why I didn't see all this before?"

"If only I could get some hard evidence on him, even if it were something which did not point directly to a conspiracy and his election. I might be able to use it just to try and stop him."

"Let's see. Electronic Images Incorporated's main headquarters, and largest complex of offices and assembly buildings, is somewhere outside of Phoenix if I remember correctly. I wonder if there are any illegal activities going on there? If nothing else, since it is the only authorized contractor of electronics to the government, perhaps a look at their books might reveal something."

"The next question seems to be: 'How does one go about doing that?' "

He leaned back in his chair and thought for quite a while before it occurred to him. He remembered that he had once had a friend and supporter on the Washington Post by the name of Tom Segal.

Segal had always been an admirer of investigative reporters who broke the famous scandals of the seventies and eighties. He had a particular sort of hero worship for Woodward and Bernstein. He had not so secretly wished to land a news breaking story of historic importance himself, but had never succeeded partly due to a lack of opportunity coupled with a certain lack of finesse.

Butler wondered if he was still with the Post, if he still had his "snooping" ambitions, and how much the F.C.C. regulations now limited his activities. He decided to call him.

"This time I'm using a public videophone," he commented to himself.

He told Mary that he was taking a lunch break and that he would be gone for a while and to record his video messages. He went out on foot in search of a public videophone which was sheltered enough to give some privacy.

He found a sit-down-one with a closing outer door not more than a block away. These were generally used by people who had either lots of business to transact or those calling long distance. They also had the advantage of being air-conditioned. The other type, the stand-up-ones, were usually used by people for short calls such as summoning commuters or making quick appointments. These were neither private nor air-conditioned.

Sitting down he accessed the videophone. An operator in uniform appeared. "Yes, Sir. How may I help you?"

Having used a public videophone so seldom, Butler had forgotten that there was an intervening operator. "Get me the Washington Post, please."

"Please enter your bank code and Social Security Number," she commanded.

"Crap! Something else I had forgotten about!" he thought as he followed directions.

The main operator for the Washington Post appeared next on the screen. "Washington Post. What department and whom shall I say is calling?" she asked with a nasal quality to her voice.

"Well, er, I am not sure which department. I am trying to contact a Tom Segal. He used to work for the City Desk."

"He still does. I'll see if he is in. What was your name, Sir?"

"Butler, Senator Butler," he hesitantly told her.

After a brief pause, and some static and interference, the picture and sound once again cleared and focused on a plumpish looking man, somewhere in his late fifties with silver hair, beard and mustache. He somewhat resembled a jolly Santa Claus. Apparently, through the years, he had most likely wined and dined liberally.

Butler did recognize him with some difficulty and thought to himself before addressing the image, "I hope he hasn't become too fat and lazy!"

"Tom. Tom Segal. You remember me?"

"Sure! Senator Butler, er, Richard. You haven't changed a bit except maybe for the gray hair. How are you? What can I do for you?"

"Well, it has been such a long time, Tom, that I thought it was about time to get together after all these years. I still am very grateful for all your help and support. I happen to have a couple of free hours for a change and would really like to renew acquaintances over lunch."

As he was speaking, Butler first flashed a very quick sign with his forefinger pressed against his lips signaling confidential matters. Then he winked at each period of his sentences to attempt to further convey that there were hidden meanings to his words. He only hoped that Segal was alert enough to catch on and that he didn't think that he simply had something caught in his eye."

He was immediately reassured when Segal returned a couple of his winks and gave an almost imperceptible nod of his head as he answered, "That would be great, Richard. I'd love to catch up on what has been going on in your life and chew over old times. I can get away in about ten minutes. How about meeting at the place we used to years ago? You know, the one with the outdoor patio?"

"That would be fine. See you there in thirty minutes," and Butler deactivated the videophone.

At that same moment, an oversized black transporter

van slipped around the corner from where Butler had been making his videocall.

Inside, one of the technicians turned to another one and observed, "First data we've picked up on the Senator. He seldom turns on his videoscreen. Obviously, from his behavior, he may be up to something, but we have no recorded proof of any violation so far."

The second technician, seemingly in a bad mood, retorted, "First of all what is so unusual about meeting an old friend for lunch? Man you could find something suspicious in a new born baby's first cry. I swear! According to his background file, Segal used to help him by covering him favorably and even slipping in a few pieces in the editorial section. Of course, that was before the F.C.C. had control over all the media. He helped the Senator get elected and reelected in the old days. He owes him a lot!"

"Sounds innocent enough, but it could have been a cryptic message of some sort," persisted the first technician. "Besides, Segal is on one of our standby monitoring lists because of earlier activities."

"Yes, but it is also true that during the past few years he appears to have been following the rules, been detached from political involvement, and simply has been doing his prescribed job."

"Well, I know one thing for sure. If he continues to renew contact with Butler, he may be moved to the active list."

"If, as you say, it was a cryptic message, why didn't the encephalogram pick up something?"

"There was time to barely begin recording before he deactivated. Doesn't prove a thing!"

"Well, even if we had any evidence of 'improper thought', our orders are to gather evidence, and to hold off on detention until we receive instructions to the contrary. You can surely see that this discussion is moot on all counts for Christ's sake!"

"Better watch that kind of talk Mister or you'll be

next!"

"Yea? You and who else is going to make . . ." and his voice trailed off as the van rolled on.

At exactly the same time Butler left the cube and began his progress towards his rendezvous. He thought of hopping the monorail, but decided he'd get there too soon. Instead, he went part way by moving sidewalk.

As agreed, they met in a noisy outdoor patio not far from the Botanic Gardens and only two blocks off of Independence Avenue. Even though the place was in the heart of D.C., the two knew that it was not popularly frequented by politicians and their staffs.

It was more of a tourist place, catering to those on low budgets without expense accounts. It still had the "old-fashioned" kind of food whereas many of the fast places had meal pills that were swallowed with water and only took a few minutes of one's time.

When a waiter asked them what they wanted, Butler just ordered dehydrated coffee as he was in no mood to eat. On the other hand, Segal ordered a "Washington Special" which was a full course, old-fashioned meal.

"Would you like to see our pill menu?" inquired the waiter turning his attention to Butler.

"No. Just bring me a coffee powder," he answered. "If alcohol was still available openly and legally, I'm sure Tom would be having several martinis first," Butler thought. "Maybe this is one time I am thankful for it being on the Federal Controlled Substance and Narcotics Table."

While waiting for Segal's meal to be delivered, he added hot water to his powder, sipped his coffee, and briefly related his theories, fears and possible plans. He admitted that most of the evidence upon which all this was founded was circumstantial, but fairly convincing nevertheless.

As he talked, he automatically checked to be sure that no one was close to their table that either looked suspicious or might be listening.

"Boy, am I getting paranoid!" he stated with a dry chuckle.

"From everything you've told me, probably with good reason, Richard. I am wondering if I should even be talking to you at this point," Segal answered half kidding.

"Tom, if you don't help I won't have anyone else I can turn to. I don't even trust my colleagues or anyone at the House. I don't know how they are doing their spying and other things, but I am sure that they are doing it!" He then outlined his ideas about Electronic Images Incorporated.

"Listen, you know as well as I do that I've always wanted to uncover some sordid tale of corruption in government, but the time for that has probably passed. Even if I did find out anything, I could not publish it. You know the rules!" Segal said half sadly, yet with a dreamy look in his eyes which indicated that a part of him was imagining what it would be like or might be considering the possibilities.

"At this point, I am not asking you to publish anything. I simply want you to do a little investigating to see if we can find out anything. If you do get some hard evidence, then I'll figure out what to do with it. Chances are if it is to be published, I'd have to hand it to the foreign media."

Segal thought about the whole thing for a while and then said, "You realize that the complex in Arizona is right out in open desert? There would be no way to break in. Since they are the largest and practically only electronics company approved by the government for several products, their security must be impenetrable."

"Well, I sort of figured that," answered Butler on the edge of sarcasm. "There must be some other way."

"It seems to me that the only way to get inside would be to infiltrate and make it appear legitimate."

"What do you mean?" Butler queried.

"I mean that myself, or someone stupid enough to try it, would have to apply and get a job in the place. Once in, they might be able to do some snooping although I am sure it would be limited."

"That wouldn't work. They use your Social Security file and number to access your Life Transaction dossier which, I am sure, lists your job as a reporter and your whole history. Even if they were not suspicious of your job, your background alone would get you rejected."

Looking as though he was beginning to consider the project as a challenge, an attitude that might overrule his original pragmatic assessment of the situation, Segal answered with excitement, "Aha! There is a way to get around that! I've done it several times before in simpler situations."

Looking surprised at both the statement and the mounting excitement which sounded in his voice, Butler inquired, "Really? What would you do?"

"Simple, find a Social Security file and number of someone who resembles me physically, and who has some skills needed for the job, and use it instead of mine."

"God! It might work, but of course, I don't have to tell you that, that is a major crime. If you got caught, you'd be put away for life at the very least!" stated Butler rather alarmed. "Does this mean that you are considering doing it yourself?"

"I am afraid that the old excitement of the hunt, so to speak, is rather appealing. I know that, at first, I wasn't interested in sticking my neck out even for something as potentially exciting and possibly as important as this. I probably have little chance of having any effect on whatever is really going on, but I'll never know if I don't give it a try, right?"

Still surprised at the sudden enthusiasm, Butler simply shook his head.

"What is more, I am getting old and I am in poor health basically. I most likely don't have a whole lot of time left. The drinking I used to do has practically destroyed my liver and I have had several heart attacks. They refused to take me on as a candidate for heart repair or artificial replacement. Same with the liver. I guess they figure I am too old and not important enough to waste the time and the money," he reasoned out loud.

"At any rate, I really don't have much to lose. Perhaps I could still attempt to contribute something to this country by trying to help. Who knows, if successful it may be something I'd be remembered for. Sort of brings back the old days. It could give my remaining life some meaning! Sure I'll do it. Thanks for talking me into it."

"Sounds like you talked yourself into it," Butler replied, "but I am grateful whatever the reasons. There is another problem. If you are going to try and find something, it has to be soon. We'll need to act before the upcoming elections. Also, how do we know that they may be looking for someone to work for them?"

"Well, that is one advantage of working on a newspaper. Electronic Images has advertisements almost daily for quite a few positions. They also list the qualifications needed and to which plant and state to apply. It won't take but a few minutes to decide on what job to go for."

"That's great! Can you get away? I mean, how are you going to explain it at your work?" he wanted to know.

"That's easy. I have some vacation coming, and in addition I often take off for medical reasons. It will just seem routine. As soon as I have it arranged, I will take the Western Shuttle."

Looking alarmed Butler warned him, "Better rent a travel vehicle if you want to keep a low profile. Also, I would suggest that you buy a Money Draft at a public Computer Transaction Bank and not use your personal computer. That way you won't have to give your Social Security file and number as long as you don't travel outside the country. Even though they'll need your bank code, it will bring far less attention."

Segal with a certain amount of surprise and admiration in his voice said, "Richard, looks like you may be in the wrong business! Should have been a spy!"

"If they catch me, that's probably what they'll call me! I will stay in Washington during the break and you can reach me at home. It would be better not to call my office directly unless absolutely necessary. When you call the house, leave some sort of a message. When I have determined it is you, I'll contact you through a public videophone. Probably not really safe either, but better than my private machine."

"Guess you are right. Tell you what. I'll leave a message to call your office. I'll say that John needs to get in touch with you. I'll deactivate the video portion. It will help a little. By the way, what will your family say?" Segal wanted to know.

Trying to sound truthful, but not succeeding too well, he answered, "Oh, they are already on vacation. Guess I won't be able to join them right away as I had planned. How's Mrs. Segal, Joan, going to take all this? Can you keep her out of it?"

With a sad expression momentarily appearing in his eyes, he answered, "Oh no problem. Joan passed away five years ago. She was in poor health too."

"Sorry, Tom. I didn't know!" he paused for a moment letting the news sink in and then continued, "I'd better get back to the office now. I really don't know how to begin to thank you. Let's hope it won't be in vain!" he added as he shook Segal's hand and walked briskly away. He hopped a moving sidewalk located directly outside the restaurant and headed back towards Independence Avenue.

He left Tom eating his way through his huge lunch. He was thinking to himself, "You'd think I wouldn't be hungry at this point. Should have taken a lunch meal pill, but old habits die hard—in fact they'll kill you! Might as well enjoy it while I can," he added on a more cheerful note.

He then smacked his lips, licked a couple of fingers, emitted a loud belch, and went back to finishing his meal while several members of a family at another table stared at him with disgusted fascination.

Chapter X

SEARCHING

With dark thunderclouds hanging heavily and threateningly in the mid morning sky outside of Phoenix, Tom Segal pulled his vehicle into the visitors' storage area. In spite of the ominous sky, it was still close to one hundred and fifteen degrees outside.

Before getting out, he surveyed the area with the expert eye of a longtime reporter. He was about twenty miles outside of Phoenix off the road that eventually led to the Salt River and the Indian restricted area. It had once been a reservation, but now, as with all other restricted areas, no one was allowed on or off the premises without special passes.

As far as he could see, and his eyes were still in good shape with the help of viewing aids, there were high wire fences lining the perimeter of several square miles of multi-colored cement block buildings. Each building complex was of a different color and was separated from others by the high fences.

"Most likely they are electrified," thought Segal.

Each complex seemed to have only one entrance through the fence and each such gate was coded with a letter and a number. Only the Personnel Building's gate was actually named as such.

"They just have to give you a map and a code book to find your way around this place," he mumbled to himself.

He noticed that there were what looked like video cameras everywhere. They were at the entrances to all the gates, they hung periodically from the fences, they hung by each door of each building, and some even floated out in space about six feet off the ground possibly held up by wires or magnets. The space mounted cameras periodically roamed at will and changed positions as if they had a mind of their own.

Still before getting out of the vehicle, he noticed that a series of cement paths joined one building to the next and crisscrossed elsewhere within a complex in a random fashion.

As he was about to ask himself what these might be for, the answer was revealed almost immediately. Air transporter carts zoomed out of certain buildings and whooshed quickly to others disappearing inside through barely visible doorways. These carts were sometimes driven by live humans, but just as often by robots or at least there were humanoid-like machines perched in the drivers' seats.

Mixed in among the carts at the sides of the pathways robots on wheels occasionally exited one building, made their way along the path to the next building and then entered. Some carried fairly heavy loads of equipment such as packing boxes while others carried tools and still others carried what looked like electronic parts.

"Well that explains that," Segal said aloud. "Good thing I didn't try to break in. I'd have probably been caught in two seconds flat!"

He mopped his forehead with a dirty rag which some old timers would have recognized as a handkerchief although these were no longer made. He finally got out of the vehicle and slowly made his way toward the gate at the entrance to the Personnel Building.

There he was interrogated by a bodyless voice and a video camera which followed his every move. He answered all the questions by telling it that he had come to apply for Job Code 2152, Primary Level Sanitation Clerk. After a pause, the gate clicked open and he walked up to the building.

He had applied for that particular job because he

thought that cleaning up and emptying trash in many areas would give him the mobility he needed and the access to several buildings. In addition, it was advertised as a night shift, so most likely there would be fewer people around.

He approached the reception desk still drying his forehead although it was considerably cooler inside. A rather plain middle-aged woman with short cut hair, a detectable mustache, and viewing aids asked, "May I help you?" Her job tag designated her as "Receptionist/ Interviewer."

Segal looked around, and since there was no one else in sight, he thought it a rather redundant question as she must have known why he was there. After thinking it over, he surmised that perhaps the security section didn't automatically inform Personnel each time someone came to apply for a job.

"Yes. As I told the camera out there, I am here to apply for Job Code 2152."

"Your Social Security number, please, er, Mr.?" she asked.

"That would be 10088-2468-54332A and the name is Robert Walker," he replied trying to appear as though he were telling the truth.

The receptionist/interviewer typed the information into her computer and after a minute turned and said, "Well, Mr. Walker, according to your files, you are way overqualified for the job. Are you sure you have the right code?"

"Yes. You see I have developed some physical problems, particularly my eyesight, which makes it very difficult to do the work I used to. I believe that I can handle the sanitation work without difficulty. It would be good for my arthritis to move around. Can't sit in one place too long."

Except for the eyesight, Segal was telling the truth about his physical condition. Had he told the whole truth, however, they would never have hired him.

"I see," she answered. "It will be a little while before we let you know. Why don't you go into the viewing room over there and watch the videoscreen if you wish. You will also find some refreshments."

Following her suggestion, he walked into the small room. One wall was almost taken up by a giant videoscreen which was already blaring. There was only one chair in the place. It looked comfortable as it was padded and contoured. "You don't see these much now a days," he commented to no one in particular.

Just prior to sitting down and watching the screen, he became rather suspicious. He had heard that lie detector tests were a routine part of any job application. Why hadn't they done one on him? He guessed that perhaps this could be some sort of surprise test.

"If you could give the test without the subject's awareness, you would get a more valid one," he theorized.

"That chair sure looks unusual. Probably hiding all sorts of electrodes," he thought. "Must keep my mind blank. That way they won't know that I have been lying."

All these decisions were made in an instant. He sat in the chair and concentrated on thinking of a rock in the middle of the desert. That was the first image that popped into his mind and he held on to it.

In a large, hidden room next door, a technician exclaimed to Miss Archer, the interviewer, "Hell I've never seen results like these. The same pattern over and over and the computer reads it as, 'rock, rock, rock . . .'! Are you sure he isn't mentally impaired? I've only seen this sort of pattern with severe brain damage of various sorts! Epileptics sometimes register this sort of a pattern!"

"There is no record of that type of problem in his files. Besides, his actions and speech seem perfectly normal! Anyway, how much talent do you need for sanitary work? Maybe the electro-encephalograph is an anomaly or maybe he is daydreaming or half asleep," she suggested.

"Well, I know one thing for damn sure! He isn't watching the videoscreen. The political program we run, although it may appear to be in the normal broadcasting mode, is a carefully prepared tape to elicit emotions and opinions especially of a political and loyalty nature. Except for the cases I just mentioned and perhaps certain psychotics, it is almost infallible."

"Well, I can't have him wait forever. Shall I give him the go ahead?" Miss Archer asked.

"I guess so. He will be monitored every so often anyway. If there is a problem, we'll run across it sooner or later."

She left the hidden room, went and retrieved Segal, and then sat down behind the reception desk once again. "Well, congratulations Mr. Walker. We are awarding you the job on a trial basis. If things work out, you will become permanent in six months," she added.

She reached down somewhere behind the counter and emerged with a plastic box and something that looked like a doctor's pager. Segal noticed that both the box and the little gadget were blue and were labeled, "Blue Complex Only".

"This box contains your full uniform," she said and pointing to the little blue pager, she added, "This device is an electronic coder that contains the codes necessary to enter those buildings for which you will be responsible. It will set off a general alarm if you attempt to use it on any area other than the Blue Complex. You will report to work at twenty-one hundred hours. At that time someone will show you where to pick up your coder and will take you through your area of responsibility."

"Any questions?" she wanted to know as she handed him the blue box.

He looked at a name plate sitting on the desk, "No Miss Archer. Thank you," and he walked away retracing his steps back to his vehicle.

He had rented a room in a private household where he had his own hygieneum and entrance. There were countless ads in the papers for such accommodations. Families often added to their incomes in that way. These arrangements were cheaper, offered more privacy, and often were more comfortable than public hotels. They also gave the added advantage allowing the rent to be paid from day to day without reservations or commitments as to any particular length of stay.

Segal unpacked the plastic box. It contained a bright blue uniform including boots and a cap. "I might have guessed," he chuckled looking at the color.

He realized that he was very tired. He was surprised that with his poor physical condition he didn't feel worse. He decided to take a long nap after which he would swallow a couple of meal pills, and then get ready for work.

At exactly twenty-one hundred hours, he was met at the Personnel gate by a man also dressed all in blue.

"Mr. Walker?" he asked.

"Yes, but call me Robert," he answered.

"O.K. Robert. You can just call me Paul. Follow me and I'll show you around," he added as they skirted the Personnel Building and headed for a large square one which was most unusual as it was the only one that was not painted a bright color. It was simply the natural color of the cinder blocks of which it was made.

"This is where you will always start your shift, Robert. If you do not start and return to this building and press your coder each time, a general alarm will sound and you will be detained," he instructed.

"Damn! Everything sets off general alarms. I bet I'll set some off accidentally until I get the hang of it!"

"Better if you don't! Anyone who sets off five alarms within a month is automatically fired if, that is, there is no breach of security!"

"Shit! What are they making here anyway? You'd think it was sort of a secret weapon or something!" Segal exclaimed.

Paul stopped him in the open on their way to the

sand colored building. He lowered his voice as he said, "You don't know the half of it! At any rate, if you want to stay out of trouble, the less you know the better! If you have to discuss something and are afraid of being intercepted, there are only two places where it may be relatively safe. As far as I know, this is one dead area right here."

"The other is the Northwest corner inside of the cafeterium. Anywhere else, you'd better talk only when necessary and make sure it is only the usual expected small talk. Whatever else you do, try not to deviate from your assigned routine in any way. I am telling you this to save you from setting off alarms and eventually losing your job. I can see you look like you really need it. Besides, we always clue in new workers if we can, otherwise they would have to hire new people every week and we'd work extra hours showing them around."

"I really appreciate it, Paul. Thanks so much," said Segal really feeling very grateful especially since he didn't want get caught and this information was vital to achieving that goal.

Once again they stopped, and this time at the entrance to the building. To the right was a large computer console with slots and coded buttons. Paul pressed one above a slot labeled "Blue Complex". A voice boomed, "Social Security number Please!" After Segal gave it, the coder for the Blue Complex shot out of a slot.

As Paul grabbed it and handed it to Segal, he reminded him, "You must pick up and replace your coder here at the beginning and end of each shift or you'll set off a general alarm."

They entered the building and were confronted by a series of doors set in the walls. Each door was of a different color, and a handful of men in black uniforms carrying lazer weapons stood at the entrance to each. They did not speak to them, but Segal figured that they were the security mèn that searched the workers as they came off their shifts.

"My God! There's enough security to guard some sort of super weapon or something!" Segal thought. "It's got to be more than preventing simple industrial spying!"

With a gentle shake of one of his shoulders, Paul interrupted his thoughts and led him over to the blue door. He clicked his electronic coder twice and the door opened automatically revealing a walkway that went off into the night. A blue line marked the way.

Paul said, "Always click your key twice to start the shift and twice when you are done or otherwise . . ."

Segal interrupted with, "Yea, let me guess. Or I'll set off a general alarm, right?"

"Right."

Inside the doorway, there was a blue trash transporter air cart which held a very large bag. They both mounted the cart and Paul showed Segal how it worked. He was told that it was programmed to automatically take Segal to each building on his route in a set order. All he had to do for each section of the trip was to push the button on his coder. He did so, and the air cart noiselessly followed the blue line on the walkway and took them to the first blue building where it stopped.

They dismounted and entered it after having signaled. Inside, there was an assembly belt. Several robots added one specific part to an almost finished videoscreen machine. In this case, they were adding a mini circuit board.

In the next building, Segal noticed that the robots were adding cathode tubes to the chassis of the videoscreen machines. He asked Paul, "Don't any live people work here other than us?"

Before answering, he dragged him to a particular corner of the assembly room and pointed to the cameras, and whispered, "Remember what I said?"

Segal shook his head and then whispered back, "Sorry!"

He went on in a lowered voice, "Oh, they do in the daytime, but the night shift work is so routine the robots handle almost all of it. Of course, there are lots of security people, but you don't see them all the time."

Each successive building was the same. One single component was added to one particular electronic machine. Segal recognized videoscreen machines, shuttle security machines, and videophones. Seeing nothing unusual or out of the ordinary, Segal once again thought that there was much too much security for such simple and rather common products. He still wondered what other secrets might be buried somewhere in the huge labyrinth.

He was shown how to suction any loose particles of dust from off the floor or the assembly line. When he was through in an assembly room, he had to empty the contents of the suction machine into a special metal container which, he was told, the security people examined before it was removed.

A few buildings, which had offices with desks and where people worked or where supervisors were in charge during the day, did have trash collectors. All papers were already shredded, but it was to be Segal's job to take the 'lettuce', as they called it, and empty it into a special trash bag on his transporter air cart. It was also his job to empty the trash in the cafeterium in the same manner.

Suddenly a bell rang twice. Segal paled and looked at Paul who looked unperturbed. "That's the first break signal! Not an alarm. You'd recognize the alarm, believe me. It is a siren and shrieks in one continuous wail!"

As they entered the cafeterium, Paul led him to the Northwest corner which he had described earlier. They sat at a small table as men in different colored uniforms started to enter and sit down. Most were workers, but mixed in with these were security men in their black uniforms. Segal figured that they must be a small contingent of the security force which was taking a break.

He noticed that meal pills, dehydrated drinks, and even some fresh food could be gotten from vending machines whose displays were set into the walls very much like the experimental automats of several decades ago, although these appeared much more sophisticated and artificial. What is more, these only accepted bank electronic activity cards for payment.

Prior to introducing Segal to the others in the place, Paul whispered, "This is the only other dead area in the place. Remember, if you need to carry on a confidential conversation, this is relatively safe. Come, I'll introduce you," and with that he led Segal over to several of the other tables. Segal noticed that he made no attempt to communicate with those in black and generally ignored them.

In a few minutes another bell rang three times. Paul turned to Segal and explained, "That is the signal to go back to your shift. At the end of your work period, you will hear one long bell. That tells you that your shift is over and that you must return immediately to the Work Distribution Building. That was the one where we started. There you will be searched. After that, return your coder to the correct slot, and then you will be free to go home. Any questions?"

As he indicated there were none, Paul accompanied him on the rest of his workshift. As Segal went from building to building, he began to understand the layout and how things worked.

First, he noticed that the Blue Complex seemed to be a final assembly area for videoscreen machines, videophones, and video detection systems used for shuttle security.

All the buildings seemed to be compartmentalized so that only one step in the process was done in each one. For example, in Building 1A, chassis were assembled, in 1B cathode tubes were added, in 1C certain transistors were attached, in 1D a circuit board was added and so forth. Segal thought that this was probably done in part for security reasons and in part to keep the process simple enough so that robots could handle a lot of the work.

He was just about to head for the last building in his complex, a much larger building than all the rest when the final bell rang. Paul and he rode quickly back to their point of origin for the evening. He clicked his coder twice, was searched, and then returned the coder to the slot.

"Thanks so much for all your help, Paul. I really appreciate it," and he really meant it.

"Sure thing. Tomorrow you are on your own and I am back to my regular shift. I'll probably see you in the cafeterium." He looked at Segal for a minute, then added, "You feeling all right, Robert? You look pale."

"Oh, just a little tired. I'll be okay. By the way we missed the last building. Any problem with that?" Segal wanted to know.

"No. It's okay if you don't finish once in a while. When you get the hang of things you'll get to it easily and may even have time left over."

"That's good to know. Thanks again, Paul."

"My pleasure. See ya!" and he walked off towards his vehicle as Segal did the same.

In the middle of the night, Segal was suddenly awakened by pain in his chest. These were rather familiar to him as they had preceded two heart attacks. He was warned that he might not live through the next one. Breaking out in a cold sweat, he carefully got out of bed and began to rummage through his travel kit.

"God. I almost thought I'd forgotten them," he said as he uncapped a large bottle of multicolored pills and swallowed several. He lay back down on the bed and after a while the pain subsided.

"Guess I'll live a few more hours," he thought as he rolled over and went back to sleep.

The next evening, he was still tired, but feeling a little better than the night before as he reported back to the gate and the work building.

As he went to work, he felt disappointed that after all his efforts, he had no access to general offices. In fact he had no idea where they were. The few desks that he ran across in his buildings were simply those of supervisors and had nothing to do with the main workings of the company. He was still convinced that the massive security must be for some important purpose he had yet to discover.

That evening he got through all the same buildings in his complex as he had the day before with Paul. He finally entered the last very large one that he had had to skip the night before. It was in there that all finished appliances eventually ended up just prior to packing and shipping.

It was divided into three very large sections one for videoscreen machines, one for videophones, and the third for shuttle security video machines. When totally assembled, all three types of sets proceeded into one final room on converging conveyer belts. They came out the other end packed and ready for shipment. There was no clear sight of the inside of the final room although robots occasionally entered through a single door.

Thinking that perhaps he was acting contrary to the advice he was given by Paul, he peeked into the room. He noticed that before adding the final cover to each appliance, the robots installed what looked like a very tiny video camera.

"Uh! I've never seen anything like that before!" he said to himself. "Wonder what it is for? I've taken videoscreen machines apart and don't remember anything like that."

He decided that when he got the chance, he would ask Paul about it. He hoped that he could be trusted and wasn't an inside 'plant', but thought he would just have to take that chance.

Later that night, when the bell had sounded the break, Segal motioned Paul over to the table in the dead area. "Say Paul," he started. "Have you ever seen that little black thing that looks like a tiny videocam that they put in all the sets?"

Paul immediately appeared alarmed and looked around him before answering, "Yes, but its use is highly classified. I've heard rumors, but that's all. I would suggest you drop the subject!"

"Rumors? What kind of rumors?" Segal wanted to know.

"Well it supposed to have something to do with surveillance. That's how they monitor us here I was told. I've even heard that that little thing can record brain waves which can be translated into thoughts by computer. That's all I am going to say! You realize that discussing this puts us in danger and especially if there is any truth to it!"

Segal paused for a moment letting the concept sink in and thinking, "Is it possible? Why in all the appliances? You don't suppose that they have been in sets for months now or even a year or two? Could that explain the mysterious arrests Butler was talking about? I've got to get ahold of one and have it checked."

Out loud he said, "Thanks Paul. You bet I will drop the subject. Wouldn't want to get either of us into trouble," and with that he went back to work at the ring of the bell.

As he started the end of his shift, he felt the old familiar chest pain. This time, it was accompanied with a few irregular beats which made him cough. He reached inside his shirt, pulled out his pills, and making sure his back was towards any cameras, he swallowed a couple. They took a little longer to do any good, but finally the pain stopped. He wiped his forehead and returned to his work.

"I could try and smuggle one of those things out in my trash bag. They only check it after I am searched and leave the Work Distribution Building," he thought.

As he got to the last building, he did the routine things first. Leaving one last trash collector to be emptied, he marched into the last room with one of the robots. He matched every movement to that of the robot hoping that if any cameras were turned towards him, perhaps they wouldn't notice him at first. When the robot placed the minicamera into the appliance and was ready to tighten the two screws, Segal picked it up and palmed it, but replaced the two screws so that the robot went ahead and tightened them without missing a beat.

He then doubled up with another robot that was leaving the room. He dropped the device into the trash collector and then emptied the collector into the large bag on his transporter air cart.

He made his way back to the Work Distribution Building and parked the cart. There was a perimeter fence not ten yards from where he was standing, so he quickly retrieved the black minicam and hurled it as hard as he could over the fence into the darkness in the direction of the vehicle storage area.

Fleeting pains licked at his chest again, as he made his way towards his vehicle and got in. He swung it around so that the lazer lights pierced the dark in the direction where he thought he had thrown the minicam.

"Aha! Sure enough, there it is! Now if I can just swoop past it and pick it up without appearing to stop, maybe I can get away with this."

He matched action to his words, and was soon on his way back to Phoenix. Again, his heart beat irregularly, but a few more pills seemed to correct the situation, at least for the moment.

"I must get back to Washington immediately. Who knows if they were watching me or if they record things and check the tapes later. Better go while I can. For a while, they will be searching for Robert Walker. Until they find out that someone took his name and number, I should be safe. The way this ticker is acting is another good reason for a quick retreat to Washington. I hope I can make it!"

He drove back stopping only to rest and additionally whenever his chest pains returned. It only took him three days as during most of the trip his vehicle was on automatic and could reach and maintain speeds close to a hundred and fifty miles an hour.

"I must call Butler and leave the agreed upon message," Segal thought as he urgently looked around for a public videophone cube.

As he reached one the familiar pain grabbed his chest with a new vengeance. He was afraid that he might not have the time to wait for Butler's return call, so he accessed the Senator's office directly. Unfortunately, he was not in so he had to leave a message—safe or not!

With practically superhuman will, he painfully made his way back to his vehicle. He had to get home and rest for a few hours or he felt he wouldn't be of use to anyone!

Chapter XI

STRUGGLING

Early one morning in mid-September Senator Butler punched the message retrieval button on his videophone. A blank videoscreen appeared with a written message underneath.

The message said, "John calling. Meet me at same place as last time around 1600 hours. Urgent!" For some reason, he had not left the message at his home as they had agreed. This both puzzled and alarmed him.

Butler knew that he meant that they were to meet at the same outdoor restaurant off of Independence Avenue and he felt a mixture of curiosity and anxiety. "He must have uncovered something important by the sound of it. Why did he call the office?"

He looked at the crystal timepiece on the wall of his office just as it said, "Nine hundred hours in the year 2016." Butler thought that he would have a hard time waiting those seven hours, but he must manage somehow.

As the day wore on and he got caught up in the routine of his day, he was surprised to hear the timepiece announce that it was fifteen-thirty hours. "Better make for the place in case he is early," he thought.

He told Mary to take his messages, grabbed his coat, and headed out on foot. This time he hopped the monorail heading toward the stop near the restaurant.

When he arrived, he spotted Segal at a table which again was isolated and in a corner.

As he sat down, Butler noticed that he looked terrible. He was sweating profusely, even though the day was not a hot one, he was very pale, he seemed to be having difficulty breathing, and he was slumped in his chair at an unusual angle.

"Hi, Tom. Are you feeling all right?" he asked.

Shaking his head, Segal answered in an almost inaudible voice and between breaths, "Afraid not. It's the old heart! I had to see you before I call an emergency transporter. Not much time. I found this thing at Tower's company. Seems they've been putting them in video products for a long time now. Rumor has it that it can record brain waves and then read them," and with that he handed over the little black camera-like device to Butler.

Letting what he just heard sink in, he first of all quickly put the black device in one of his inside pockets then said, "Good work Tom. That would explain a lot if it is true! You'd better get ready to go. I'll go find a videophone."

"No wait! I know of someone who is an electronic whiz! She has worked for me on several stories and is reliable, I'm sure. Here is her name and address. I will leave first and find a videophone. You wait until I have gone before you go anywhere. Try to get the thing to Sharon Lambert as soon as possible. God knows if they can trace it somehow. Good luck." He got up slowly and painfully. Clutching his chest with one hand and supporting himself against walls and furniture with the other, he labored out of the patio and into the street.

Holding on to the walls of buildings, Segal tried to separate himself as far as he could from the restaurant. As soon as he made a call, he would get on the moving sidewalk and lay down if he must. He felt his heart beating irregularly and he began to cough finding it impossible to catch his breath. The pain now radiated down his left arm and into the fingers of his hands. He looked around desperately searching for a videophone.

Just as he spotted one, two members of the People's Police grabbed him saying, "You are under arrest Mr. Segal alias Robert Walker!"

By way of an answer, Segal grabbed his chest one final time, let out a yell of pain, began turning blue, and expired in such a way that the two policemen were holding a corpse whether or not they realized it at that moment.

Feeling the dead weight, one officer finally turned to the other and said, "You know I think this man is dead!"

The other answered, "Well, it looks like he saved us a lot of trouble. Let's call this in."

They dropped the corpse right there on the non-moving part of the sidewalk as they signaled for an emergency transporter. Passers-by stared in horror, but did not dare to make any comments. They simply floated by on the moving part of the sidewalk as if silent ghostly spectres witnessing some incomprehensible human drama.

After a few minutes, Butler got up and left the restaurant. Unaware of the scene taking place down the street, he hopped onto the mobile sidewalk heading back toward Independence Avenue.

He again decided to take the monorail and head immediately to the address that Segal had given him.

As he boarded the crowded car, he noticed that the location was close to where he and his family had rented the travel vehicle about a month ago.

In that time he had received one message from them through the regular mail. Although most everyone used computers and electronic mail, there were still a few old fashioned mail centers in larger cities where written letters could be picked up and sent. This small volume of mail went only to cities serviced by air shuttle. Notices were sent to addressees by electronic means telling them to come to the center and pick up their mail.

He'd been so busy that he had managed to keep his mind off of his family much of the time. When he received the letter he realized that he felt the awful pain of their absence more than he could have imagined.

Upon opening the letter, he had found out that they were doing all right, but that they too missed him very much. They were very anxious to know when he would be able to join them.

He had written back that he hoped it would be soon and had advised them to go on to Victoria Island and wait for him there. He would not be able to write, as there was no mail center there, and he was more afraid than ever to use any electronic device.

He spotted the street he wanted and got off at the next stop. He doubled back along the street bordering the now familiar restricted area and turned right onto a smaller one.

The sun was sinking in the late afternoon sky and the shadows were lengthening. Butler picked up the pace as this part of town made him nervous and he wanted to get out of it, if possible, before nightfall.

Even though it was against the law, shadowy figures of the homeless lurked in dark doorways and began furtively moving about. If they stayed too long, they would soon be rounded up in the nightly raids and would end up behind the fences of the restricted areas.

"Fortunately, I have my valid Social Security file and proof of residence and work. Otherwise, I could be taken in if I got caught out here after dark and on foot," Butler reasoned. "Of course, if on the other hand they are looking for me anyway, I could be in worse trouble if I do identify myself."

He found the electronic repair shop he was looking for which occupied a small corner of a much larger abandoned warehouse.

"I doubt that this is a government authorized business, judging by the area and the condition of the place. That's probably a good sign as Sharon Lambert is liable not to want to have much to do with the authorities. I only hope she's in," he murmured to himself.

The place was dark and the door was locked. He knocked loudly and impatiently. After a few minutes, which seemed like an hour to him, a light came on somewhere in the back.

Finally, a door opened, and a small, not very clean-looking woman in a worn out and rumpled uniform appeared. Because of the dim light, it was hard to determine what she really looked like. She asked him what he wanted.

He answered, "My name is Robert Butler. Tom Segal sent me. I need your help."

Sharon glanced quickly and nervously up and down the street, and then said, "Come in. Follow me."

He realized that the front of the store had not been used for a long time. Glancing about him, he saw that there were several inches of dust on the few broken crates and other debris strewn about. Spider webs completed the picture and helped to give him the impression that he had somehow entered an ancient movie set of some long forgotten horror show. Suddenly, he tripped on a broken chair and uttered several loud swear words.

"Be careful! Stay behind me," she cautioned as she headed for a doorway through which a light was shining.

As they entered that room Butler was both surprised and impressed. He noticed that the place was filled with the most modern of electronic equipment.

"Where did you get all this?" he asked in amazement.

"Let's just say that I have friends in the right places," she replied evasively.

As he looked around some more, he realized that the room also served as living quarters and for probably more than one person. Among the abundant odds and ends, there were several makeshift beds.

She cleared off an old chair with a broken back and offered him a place to sit. After staring at him for a few minutes as if sizing him up, she inquired as to the nature of the help he needed.

He briefly related part of the story ending up with Tom's latest discovery which he pulled out and handed to her saying, "Can you tell whether this thing can really record brain waves which can be read by computer?"

"I might be able to. Of course, I don't have the

programs that translate the recordings, but by using my computer to analyze this device, I may be able to get some clues and perhaps enough parts of the program to at least demonstrate whether it is possible."

"Will it take long?" he wanted to know. "I'd hate to get caught around here after dark."

"I'm not sure. Depends. You didn't use your vehicle? Just as well. A vehicle parked around here after dark would only draw attention. Don't worry. I have one hidden next door in the warehouse and I'll drive you back if need be. This place is secure. I have all sorts of warning devices and different ways to get out."

As she went to work, he noticed that if she were groomed and changed clothes, she probably would be rather attractive. She was petite. Her short hair was thick and brown. Her face had regular fine features. Her eyes were a deep blue and her eyelashes were naturally long and dark. Her mouth was small, but sensuous and when she opened it, it revealed perfect white teeth.

Catching himself becoming too involved and interested in her, he asked, "Sharon. Is it all right if I call you Sharon?"

Looking at him sharply as if reading his mind, she answered in a neutral tone, "Sure. Call me what you want."

"I'm curious to know how you got started in all this," he motioned around at the display of computers and other appliances.

"Look," she retorted rather tensely and impatiently, "You came here to find out something. If it weren't for Tom I wouldn't be doing this. I've agreed to, and that's all we need to discuss. If we find your theory to be true, all the more reason to keep personal information to ourselves. Agreed?"

He blushed, realizing that perhaps she had sensed his growing interest in her probably before he himself had become aware of it, and simply nodded. For just an additional fleeting moment he thought that if it had been another time, another place, then who knows? He shrugged quickly dismissing the thought.

After several hours, and as Butler's eyes kept closing and he was about to nod off, Sharon finally had something to say. "Well, I've found out that the first part, recording brain waves, can be done by the machine. This device can pick up brain wave configurations within a few yards and store them on a mini crystal. Inside is a miniature, but advanced computer along with a receiver and a transmitter. The transmitter can be activated remotely. My guess would be that translating the resulting brain wave recordings at the receiving end is quite possible. Just by logic, if the first half of the theory is true, then there is a good possibility that the second half is possible as well."

"Well, that finally clinches it! Those bastards!" He hissed through clenched teeth. "Any idea why they put in videoscreens and the like?"

"Apparently they use the broadcast signals at that particular wavelength to transmit the data. Also, they gain their extra power from the more powerful transformers. It will still record and store when the sets are off, but can only transmit when the appliance is actually up and running."

"Any way to deactivate it?" he wanted to know.

"Best way might be to try and remove it from every appliance that has a cathode tube, and of course, one that is accessible. For instance, you can't tamper with the public ones. Chances are, though, that removing it may set off a signal that could draw immediate attention. Probably the same would be true if you tried to shut it down by cutting the power source."

"What about unplugging and removing those sets you could get to?"

"As I said before, it has its own power source for recording, but it would not be able to transmit. Certainly would buy time. Moving the sets either out of the house or to an unused section of a house or office might work.

There'd be no alarm and no input. They'd eventually check when they weren't getting any recordings, though. Incidentally, when out in public, it would be wise to always concentrate on something innocuous. That way they wouldn't be able to get anything important."

"You can't imagine how grateful I am for the information and the advice. There's no real way I can repay you except to extend my sincere thanks and to let you know you can call on me anytime if ever you need to."

"I understand and I'll keep it in mind. It is almost daylight so you'd better get going! Best time to move about. Good luck! You have a hard struggle ahead of you!"

"You bet! I must find a way to stop this business and try to warn people," he said in a grimly determined way.

Taking the brain cam he asked for the printout of the analyses that demonstrated how the thing worked. It was just a long jumble of figures along with a few recognizable words and a few patterns that resembled brain wave recordings, but an expert could make sense of it. On an impulse he gave her a quick hug. He noticed that she did not resent nor resist it. She waved him out.

Dawn had arrived and the sun was peeking over the horizon as he retraced his steps back to the monorail stop. Both streets were absolutely deserted with no hint of the human shadows of the night before. The desperate had either been rounded up and removed or had found a new place to hide.

Later, Butler sensing that he had little time left, set the automatic on the console of his commuter vehicle and pondered his next, perhaps desperate and useless move as the vehicle headed towards his residence.

Chapter XII

CHALLENGING

The next morning, Senator Butler was once again in his office. "I wonder if I should check to see if Tom is all right? He really looked terrible the other day," he wondered, but then he thought it would be safer for both of them if he didn't try to contact him for the time being.

"That reminds me," he thought looking around the office. "The videoscreen and videophone must go. Wonder if the computer is safe? Probably not."

He unplugged both the computer and videophone and hauled these to a clothes closet where he put them and shut and locked the door. Looking at the built in videoscreen, he realized that it presented a bigger problem.

"I can't start taking the wall apart," he reasoned.

After a few minutes of thinking about it, he finally pulled an extra desk over to the wall and placed it beneath the videoscreen. He then piled a metal lazer disc holder on top of the desk and in front of the screen. He followed these actions by placing several other objects, in front of, and on top of, the disc holder.

"I hope that will stop that brain cam," he thought as he looked at the mess he had made which vaguely reminded him of a door that had been barricaded to prevent entry.

"Anyone who comes in here will think I've lost my mind! If I am not careful, I could end up in an R.R.P. or restricted area for being reported as mentally unfit!" he almost chuckled at the irony.

He sat at his desk and buzzed for Mary who entered

almost immediately. "Good morning, Senator. How . . ." and she paused in mid sentence staring around the office. "What's all that?" she asked pointing to his makeshift barrier, "and what happened to your videophone and computer?"

He realized that he would now have to let her in on at least part of what was going on so that she would know that there was a rationale for his actions, and that he hadn't lost his mind. In addition, he wanted her to be informed so that she could attempt to keep her office relatively secure.

So he responded with, "Mary, Close the door. Sit down. I have something important to discuss with you although I am sure that you will find what I am about to tell you somewhat hard to believe at first," and he went on to briefly outline what he knew.

As he expected, after listening to him, she was at first dumbfounded and incredulous. She stared at him with a blank expression as if trying to determine if he was actually serious. When he finally showed her the braincam and documents, she finally seemed convinced that he wasn't having delusions.

"Please put these in the safe without anyone, not even the others on the staff, seeing you," he instructed.

"Shall I unplug my videophone, computer, and cover the videoscreen in the staff office too?" she wanted to know.

"No. Better not. If the links from this office are totally broken they might, at the very least, send up a team of electronic diagnosticians to see what is wrong. It would be better to simply avoid thinking about anything vital or important, especially concerning what I told you. Someone told me that when you are near a screen, if you want to prevent being read, you can concentrate on some common object and that will help to block out other thoughts."

"All right, Senator. Anything else?"

"Yes. As soon as you have the stuff in the safe,

please punch up the Independent Council regulations to see if they still exist and in what form."

"Certainly Senator," and she returned to the staff office.

He knew that he had about one chance in a million to succeed, but he intended to attempt to start an investigation into the conspiracy no matter how poor the odds might be. Even if he could get the Attorney General's office to go through the motions, he hoped it might buy some time and slow down Tower and the others.

Mary returned a few minutes later holding several sheets of paper. "Well, we seem to be in luck if you want to use that word. They do still exist. According to these, the Attorney General can still appoint an independent council when there is evidence of malfeasance or other criminal violations by elected officials. The same goal can be achieved by a two thirds vote of the Combined House."

"That's rather ironic! They've removed people without any visible due process for violations of a bill whose criminal aspects are secret, but which is so broad and unreasonable that it can apply to anyone they choose to arrest. On the other hand, we have to be able to document and prove extensive and knowing criminal activity while in office in order to do something about their activities! If there was some way to do it, I'd be tempted to use CHB 5200 to turn the tables on them!"

"Since the Attorney General is an N.N.P.P. member herself, I doubt that I will get anywhere there, but make an appointment for me anyway. By the way, tell her I'd like to meet in one of the public lounges and not in her office," he added.

She obtained an appointment for him at eleven hundred hours. "She really thought it strange that you didn't want to meet in her office, but she reluctantly agreed," Mary told him.

"Thanks. Could you dictate legislation into your

computer, keeping it as short as possible, indicating a need for a vote on the floor for the appointment of an independent council? I sure hope that they are not monitoring draft legislation off of computers along with everything else!"

"Meanwhile, I will use the next two hours and the rest of the afternoon to inform those member of my party who are left and who can be trusted so that they'll be prepared tomorrow. I'll also work on clueing in some of the Republicans. I can't take a chance on tipping my hand by talking to the N.N.P.P.'s but hopefully, some of them may vote through ignorance if caught by surprise, and let's hope that many will be absent. It is getting close to the weekend and some will be taking off as usual. There isn't much hope, but it is worth a try."

"Let's hope so, Senator," Mary said as she once again returned to the staff office.

After talking to as many senators as he could reach, out in the hallways and away from braincams, Butler went to the lounge where the Attorney General was already waiting impatiently.

He gave her the minimum outline of a conspiracy, purposely giving her the impression that it was just a suspicion that he wanted investigated. He didn't let her know the extent of his knowledge or the evidence out of the fear that she might urgently report him to Tower's group.

As expected, she either didn't believe a word of what he said, or already knew more than she'd care to admit and consequently claimed that there was no evidence for beginning an investigation—not even a cursory, informal one. She also suggested that he needed a vacation and that he must have been working too hard.

He spent the rest of the afternoon continuing to notify as many senators as he could, picked up a copy of the legislation from Mary, and went home to his deserted house.

He set about making sure that all videophones and

computers were removed from his office, the nutrition center, the bedroom, and the hygieneum.

He screened off four videoscreens in somewhat the same manner as the one in his House office. Those were the only areas he was likely to use and he would simply stay out of the rest of the rooms.

He then made ten copies of the conspiracy scenario from beginning to end, laboriously scrawling each one by hand. He was afraid to use a computer which would have taken him only a few minutes, especially if he had used the dictation mode.

He stuffed each copy into envelopes which he also addressed by hand. It was difficult to figure out exact addresses without using either his videophone or computer, but he finally decided to direct each to a foreign capital city in which he knew there was a mail center, and to further label these to the attention of well-known foreign news services.

By the time he was through with these "trump cards", it was almost morning so he finally decided to get a couple of hours of sleep.

Later, he had Mary place the ten envelopes in the office safe alongside the braincam and other evidence.

Taking a deep breath to steady his nerves, he then headed towards the floor of the New Combined House.

"Good luck, Senator," Mary yelled after him.

By this time, the House had basically become a rubber stamp body. Anything the N.N.P.P. introduced usually passed with little or no debate. Many senators didn't even show up for some sessions, and when they did, it was often only to introduce some routine piece of legislation.

Sub-committees had long ago been disbanded so that all business was transacted on the floor of the House, and the first that most senators heard of a new bill, was when it was introduced and voted upon.

"For what purpose does the honorable Senator from Massachussetts arise?" asked the Speaker of the House.

"Mr. President. I wish to introduce CHB 6100, a request for the appointment of an independent council. I move that the oral reading be waived and I call for the question," said Butler as quickly as he could speak hoping that by some miracle the request would pass before anyone really thought about it.

"Hearing no objections, I . . ." started the Speaker.

"I object, Mr. President," interrupted Senator Wheeler who had lumbered awkwardly but with surprising speed to the microphone as soon as Butler had started to speak.

"And on what grounds, Senator?" asked the Speaker.

"First of all there isn't a quorum, Mr. President. Secondly, I wish to have the bill read which will give us some time to consider its merits," he answered.

"Mr. Speaker. It has become almost a matter of precedent that most bills have been passed with or without a quorum, without being read, and on voice votes. I cite CHB 5200 as being the first example in a long line of legislation. As a matter of fact, Senator Wheeler here was the one who shoved it through over my objections. Surely, you are not going to make an exception of this bill by changing the rules again?" Butler wanted to know.

"According to parliamentary procedure, Senator Butler, we will vote on Mr. Wheeler's request prior to voting on your legislation. The first vote should determine the manner in which your request will be considered," answered the Speaker sounding very authoritative although Butler was not so sure that he was totally impartial.

A voice vote was taken on Senator Wheeler's motion, which to Butler's surprise was defeated. Unfortunately, Wheeler's tactic had given him just enough time to send for any N.N.P.P. Senators that were in the building, and by the time the voice vote was taken on Butler's motion, there were enough votes to stop a two-thirds majority.

"Damn him. I should have tried to find a time when

Wheeler wasn't around! Just the very fact that I attempted to get an investigation started probably made him suspicious. Could he be directly involved too?" Butler wondered as he made his way back to his office.

He called Mary in and asked for the letters, the brain cam, and the documents. He explained his failed attempt, and that his last course of action was to send the letters to the foreign press and then get out of the country.

As she handed the items to him, he suggested that perhaps she should find her husband and either go into hiding or leave the country too. Working for him, and knowing what she did, most undoubtedly put her in a very dangerous position.

He hurried to the vehicle storage area, retrieved his vehicle, and pulled out into the Washington traffic. He was on his way to rent a travel vehicle planning to join his family in Canada.

At about the same time, Marshall Tower was meeting, once again and not so secretly this time, with Sean Thompson his corporate lawyer, Dick Smith of N.S.C., and Colonel Carter of F.I.A.

"You want us to pick up the little fucker?" Carter was asking referring to Butler.

"Damn right! The little bastard seems to know all about our plans and activities and just left the House after attempting to start an investigation. We've gone too far to let the meddling bastard make waves!" answered Tower.

"There is nothing that anyone can do to us at this point. We've got complete control. So why bother? He can't do anything," volunteered Thompson.

"Gentlemen! I partly agree with the lawyer here, but I see no point in leaving a token rebel running around. It just doesn't look good. It's bad for appearances. We've got just two weeks before the final election. We should keep things neat until then," whined Dick Smith ignoring or not daring to make a comment on Tower's language for the moment. "Have you got enough recordings on him yet?"

"That's the strange thing about it. He seems to also be a sneaky little bastard. He must have figured out how to avoid being recorded—at least some of the time. We have enough on him, though, to take him in. From the recordings of his secretary, we know he has a brain cam and back-up documents in his office or on his person."

"Furthermore, we know that he is in possession of several envelopes although we do not know what these are or what the son-of-a-bitch intends to do with them. We also know that he met Tom Segal just before the fucker kicked the bucket. It is just a matter of figuring out where he is and grabbing his ass. Chances are, if he has the stuff I mentioned on him, that alone would be enough to charge him without the electro-encephalographs," sputtered Colonel Carter totally forgetting, once again, to watch his language as was often requested by Smith.

"Fine Colonel. Go to it," ordered Tower, and with that, Carter left the meeting.

Turning to Thompson, Tower requested the copies of the rest of the draft bills. Thompson took a stack of paper from his briefcase and handed it to Tower.

"Dick, these are the final bills that we would like to have Wheeler introduce, and pass, in order to complete the agenda for this year. If you can talk him into it and get it done, when I am elected there will be no possibility of any challenge to our power," and with that statement Tower tried on his most sincere-looking smile.

Smith answered without even reading the papers, "I'll see to it that he gets these and that he cooperates. He did a great job this morning. I am surprised that the old coot was so much on the ball as to stop Butler without even knowing exactly what he was up to. He hasn't lost his instincts," and with those comments the three men parted company.

Richard Butler decided to make one quick stop before programming his commuter for the vehicle rental storage area he had used before. He took control of his vehicle and turned off the throughway heading towards the one Central Mail Facility that still existed in Washington.

He placed his vehicle in a short, temporary zone, and ran into the building which was pretty well deserted. It was used mainly by older people who hadn't quite converted to the electronic mail era or by people who did not have access to computers such as those who might have temporarily escaped from a restricted area, people writing to others who resided in rural areas, or by people writing to some areas overseas.

One large wall was devoted to labeled slots in which one dropped the envelopes. Each slot was named according to the mail center of destination.

He searched for a few minutes before he found a smaller section that was devoted to foreign centers. He found one for Great Britain and dropped in the appropriate envelope. Next, he found one for France and was poised to release that envelope when a gloved hand grabbed his wrist and held it.

"Got you with the evidence! You are under arrest Senator Butler!" said one of two members of the People's Police.

Prior to driving off in a People's transporter vehicle, the two had searched Butler's commuter and found the brain cam and other documents under the seat. As one of the officers turned to the other and displayed what he had found he punched in the location for Rehabilitation Plant Number One.

As they neared the throughway, he turned to the prisoner, who was totally restrained and could only move his eyes. Waving some of the documents in front of Butler's face, he said, "You won't be needing these where you are going!"

Later, standing before a judge robed in black, inside People's Internal Court Number One, Butler was still totally restrained and naked. Gone were the red and black buttons and the large computer-like devices. In their place stood one relatively small machine which had an intake device on it.

The judge spoke, "Senator Butler, we found enough evidence on you to have you stored for a long time. In addition, having conspired with a Tom Segal who illegally infiltrated a company whose efforts have been of enormous importance to the national security of this country is an additional crime that merits the limits of punishment. However, in order to make this absolutely legal, we shall now have your electro-encephalographs fed into the verdict machine. It will automatically calculate your punishments for the crimes thereon listed."

At this signal, one of the guards fed a stack of graph paper into the machine and after a few seconds, a buzzer sounded and a small paper appeared. The same guard tore it off and handed it to the judge who then read it adding his own explanations every once in a while.

"For many of the crimes already mentioned, the decision is twenty years storage. At the end of that time, disposal is required for the rest of your crimes. There obviously is to be no rehabilitation. Senator Butler, consider yourself lucky. Had all the crimes you are suspected of committing been recorded, I have no doubt that immediate disposal, what we used to call 'death penalty', would have been prescribed by the verdict machine! Consider yourself fortunate! Take him away!"

"Lucky? Fortunate? Hell! I'd choose disposal! What's the difference?" Butler asked himself as they dragged him off and he heard the judge say, "Court adjourned" just prior to the white door sliding shut.

Chapter XIII

FINALIZING

As ordered Dick Smith called Senator Wheeler into his office. He handed him a stack of draft bills and said, "Wheeler. We have a few more pieces of legislation we wish you to introduce and get passed. Judging by the control the 'Party' now seems to have, there should be no problem in getting these through."

Senator Wheeler sat silently holding the stack of papers. He no longer had any illusions whatsoever that he was being used ruthlessly. He felt very much like a trained dog that was about to be put through its paces. For a while, he seemed to be in a state of shock, but eventually, and in an automaton-like manner, he slowly flipped through and read the title of each of the documents he was holding:

CHB 6151 Designates the N.N.P.P. the Only Official Party.

CHB 6152 Military Service Requirements for Both Genders. (Part of time to be served in the People's Protective Police).

CHB 6153 Sterilization of Inferior Gene Pool.

CHB 6154 Final Nationalization of Media.

CHB 6155 Judicial Limited to Federal Courts Including Internal Courts at R.R.P.'s. Disbandment of all Local External Courts.

CHB 6156 Presidential Line Item Veto Powers.

CHB 6157 Presidential Term Unlimited.

CHB 6158 Funds Withdrawn from Public Schools. Tax Exemptions to Private Schools.

CHB 6159 Federalization of National Guard.

CHB 6160 House Veto Override Powers Deleted.

CHB 6161 Establishment of National Religion.

CHB 6162 New Priority Storage Category: Communicable Diseases.

CHB 6163 Appropriations Powers Transferred to Treasury Department.

CHB 6164 Departments of Defense and State Transferred to F.I.A. Authority.

CHB 6165 Change of Name: "President's Cabinet" to be Renamed "Central Committee".

As he read each, Wheeler's eyes widened. When through, he removed his viewing aids and with hands trembling with anger, fear and indignation, he threw the stack down on Smith's desk hissing, "You assholes must have lost your minds! I can't be a party to this business. I may have gone along in the past to help Tower get elected, but this is outrageous! It would be tantamount to handing absolute and permanent power over to the Executive Branch, and specifically to the fucking Presidency! I am not fool enough to permanently cut my own God damned throat!"

Wincing imperceptibly at the invectives and realizing that Wheeler was as angry as he could get, Smith nevertheless replied in a low, calm and controlled voice, "I'm afraid you are in too deep as it is. Either you do as we ask, or you'll end up in an R.R.P. for the rest of your life. Besides, if you won't, we can always get someone else to do the job. Be sensible and face facts. Since these will be introduced and probably passed with or without you, why not at least keep your seat?"

Looking first down at the floor, and then fixing a gaze full of hatred upon Dick Smith, Wheeler slowly gathered the stack of bills.

When he had them firmly in hand, he spat out the words, "You son-of-a-bitch!" and walked out of the office slamming the door so hard it almost came off its hinges.

Dick Smith whispered, "Temper! Temper!" after him.

Wheeler spent the rest of the time, prior to the

election, introducing the legislation all of which passed as expected.

Having finished the distasteful task the day before the Presidential Election, Wheeler, feeling like a broken man and contemplating suicide as perhaps the most honorable way out, left the floor of the House for the last time.

As he stepped through the doorway, he was promptly arrested by the People's Police.

He was hauled off as he thought to himself, "Shit! I don't believe this. It is the final insult and humiliation!"

Somehow, though, he was able to perceive some final ironic humor in his predicament as he continued to chatter, "Talk about your poetic justice! I did enough to give them power to do away with me!" and the sound of his eerie hysterical laughter echoed several times and then there was silence.

Early the next morning, dark clouds gathered in a threatening sky this time on the outskirts of Los Angeles. It was an unusual tropical storm so late in the year. It was early November and the unusual atmospheric conditions seemed symbolic of some sort of bad omen or gloomy prophecy of things to come.

Several passersby stopped to stare at an older man weaving confusedly up the street. He appeared lost and destitute. He was unshaven and disheveled and his torn and wrinkled clothes hung on him like the bandages of an ancient mummy. Dark circles accented his vacant eyes as he turned his head from side to side appearing to be searching for something.

Finally, one sympathetic woman paused to help him, asking, "Sir. Do you have an address that you wish to reach?"

The man looked at her with his glazed eyes and stayed silent.

She persisted, "If you don't get off the street, you are bound to be picked up sooner or later. Do you have any relatives? What is your name?"

The man finally had a thought and said, "I . . . er . . . I . . . Simpson, I think."

About that time two members of the People's Protective Police came upon the scene. "Step aside, lady," one of them commanded. The other asked the man, "What is your Social Security number?"

"I don't know," the man called Simpson answered.

"Where do you live?" one of the officers asked.

He just shrugged his shoulders in confusion.

One officer turned to the other and said, "This man may have been rehabilitated. He has the classic symptoms and has no papers. It is our duty to get him off the streets. Let's transport him to the nearest restricted area."

Each grabbed one shoulder as they practically carried the man, "known as Simpson" to their transporter vehicle.

The late tropical rainstorm started to disgorge its moisture and dump it upon the earth as lightning crossed the ever blackening sky. People hurried off the moving sidewalks and scattered looking for shelter from the torrential downpour.

From the open door of an enormous electronics store, the audios from several active videoscreens screamed in unison at an ungodly volume and pitch, "Tower elected by a landslide!"

THE END

(or is it?)

About the Author

Mike Rozsa was born in Brooklyn, New York. He grew up on the East Coast and spent a couple of his childhood years in France. Upon returning to the United States, he lived in New England and spent a couple of years in Concord, Massachusetts. He moved to California at the age of fourteen and spent several years in Pasadena prior to moving to Santa Barbara, California where he now resides.

He graduated from Pasadena City College with an A.A. Degree, and the University of California at Santa Barbara with both a B.A. and an M.A.

He has been an elementary school teacher since 1961—except for a three year stay in the United States Army. He has been involved in community theatre and has written and produced over twenty-five plays for elementary students. This is his first serious attempt at a book with an adult theme.